Heaven's Premier Horse Race

Brought to you by...

Eric Vaughn Floyd

Heaven's Premier Horse Race

This Book is Dedicated to

The God of Abraham

An Opening Commentary, What is Thoroughbred Horse Racing's Triple Crown Series?

What is Thoroughbred Horse Racing's Triple Crown Series? Well essentially, it is a "three act sporting theatrical" that is headlined by Planet Earth's eminent three-year old equines. Rekindled each year on the first Saturday in May at Churchill Downs in Louisville, Kentucky, the Triple Crown Series kicks off with the world's most famous horse race; the Kentucky Derby. Also dubbed "The Run for the Roses" and "The Most Exciting Two Minutes in Sports", the Kentucky Derby is disputed over horse racing's traditional "classic distance" (one and a quarter miles).

Once the curtain comes down in Louisville the Triple Crown Series shifts to Pimlico Race Course in Baltimore, Maryland. This is where, on the third Saturday in May, the Preakness Stakes takes place. Run at a mile and three sixteenths, the Preakness Stakes is popularly referred to as both "The Run for the Black-Eyed Susans" and "The Triple Crown's Middle Jewel".

Following a second hiatus (this time for three weeks instead of two), the Triple Crown Series culminates at Belmont Park in Elmont, New York. An exceptionally demanding mile and a half "marathon", the Belmont Stakes has hence been aptly nicknamed "The Test of a Champion". (Incidentally, the Belmont's arduous distance is undoubtedly the number one reason why only thirteen equines in all of history have exited Thoroughbred Horse Racing's Triple Crown Series with three corresponding blue ribbons.)

The Lead In...

On June 6th, 2015, *American Pharoah* became the first equine in thirty-seven years to complete a sweep of Thoroughbred Horse Racing's Triple Crown Series. (Then of course we have *Justify*, the racer who will forever bear the moniker of "2018 Triple Crown Champion".) Now by virtue of these historic events, "Horse Racing Nation" has entered into a perennial debate which garners its fuel via the abstract question of, "Where do they (American Pharoah and Justify) rank in terms of the eleven other Triple Crown Champions?"

Well the truth is, regardless of who comes along, it's probably impossible to supplant the legacy of the thoroughbred who won the Triple Crown back in 1973. That's because no equine has ever run the: Kentucky Derby, Preakness Stakes or Belmont Stakes faster than *Secretariat*! (Oh, and if that wasn't enough, history also shows that *"Big Red"* (that's Secretariat's informal title) romped in "The Test of a Champion" by an inconceivable thirty-one lengths!)

Despite the aforementioned résumé, some still argue that *Citation* would have given Secretariat a run for his money. Acquisitioning immortality in 1948, Citation (or *"Big Cy"*) was ridden by one *Eddie Arcaro*, a jockey who, in the context of the Triple Crown Series, has no equal. See, over a career which spanned four decades, Arcaro procured: five Kentucky Derby titles, six Preakness Stakes' titles, six Belmont Stakes' titles and two Triple Crown Championships. Reverentially christened *"The Master"* by his peers, Arcaro was also regularly quoted as saying, "He (Citation) was the best horse I ever rode."

Really, when it comes right down to it, we will never truly know how American Pharoah and Justify "stack up" until they line up against Secretariat, Citation and nine other horses named: *Sir Barton* (immortalized - 1919), *Gallant Fox* (immortalized - 1930), *Omaha* (immortalized - 1935), *War Admiral* (immortalized - 1937), *Whirlaway* (immortalized - 1941), *Count Fleet* (immortalized - 1943), *Assault* (immortalized - 1946), *Seattle Slew* (immortalized - 1977) and *Affirmed* (immortalized - 1978). Having said this, let's hope it's quite a while before American Pharoah and Justify connect with their mates on the other side of the pearly gates.

Now while a skirmish which features all thirteen Triple Crown Champions is pure fantasy, it's been rumored that our "overhead neighbors" have an actual hope of seeing a different kind of "dream race". (Yup, you guessed it, the type that would pit Heaven's eleven elite equines against one another!) Therefore, pack your toothbrush and an extra pair of undergarments my friend, for we are immediately relocating to that sanctified allotment of terra firma which crowns the core of our *Everlasting Father's* enigmatic Universe.

Chapter 1 - Paradise Farms

Nestled away inside the far southwest corner of *God's* glorious kingdom, "Paradise Farms" is where every Triple Crown Champion is transported once their mortal cycle expires. Now as of this writing, Heaven's largest equine preserve is "structurally endowed" with: eleven Mediterranean style mansions and one monstrous eleven-stall 14kt gold overlaid Primary Barn. Made up of eleven Guardian Angels (hence the eleven mansions), Paradise Farms' live-in staff is forever sworn to the following mission statement, "We Purpose Ourselves to Pamper Eternity's Prized Equines."

Proportionate in size (777 sq. ft.), those eleven stalls which make up Paradise Farms' Primary Barn are also identically furbished with: central heat and air conditioning, wall to wall hand-woven red shag carpeting, a king-sized canopied goose feather horse bed, seven wide-palm blade ceiling fans, a sparkling water reservoir, loads of organic carrots, a cedar barrel brimming with red-delicious apples, sterling silver oat and hay troughs, a Dead Sea salt lick, an electronic peppermint dispenser and a retractable stained glass skylight.

Flat out "Kings of the Castle", those stabled at Paradise Farms indeed have absolute run of the place. Thusly, Heaven's eleven Triple Crown Champions are free to: snooze past noon, forage in the properties' Core Meadow for hours on end, lounge beneath a lofty Juniper tree, take a soak in a hot mineral spring or even, recreationally duel one another. In fact, Gallant Fox and his son Omaha routinely "hook up" for a few furlongs when they are first let out in

6

the morning. The real race however occurs nightly at exactly 6:00 PM. (This is when a Guardian Angel named *Ariel* rings the dinner bell.)

It appears then that our would-be headliners are game for a formal tussle. However what about the: owners, trainers, jockeys, and grooms who helped make them famous? Well, even though these "Connections" want what the entirety of "Horse Racing Nation" wants, there has always been this perception that drafting a "Charter of Competition" would be next to impossible (on account of all the different ideas about what "Heaven's Premier Horse Race" should look like). Nevertheless, every pertinent: owner, trainer, jockey and groom got on board when "Ariel & Friends" (at the request of Horse Racing Nation) mailed out some gold leaf invitations that read,

We, the staff of Paradise Farms, extend the use of our Core Meadow
On Sunday, September 25th @ 12:00 PM
For the purpose of a Triple Crown
"Connections' Summit"
One which will hopefully spur the creation of
"Heaven's Premier Horse Race"

(A complimentary gourmet lunch buffet will be provided.)

Since his Sunday morning routine always included a 7:00 AM tee time, Eddie Arcaro literally wound up pulling his gold Jaguar into Paradise Farms' last available "guest-parking" spot at noon on the dot. Subsequent to stepping foot inside of the Core Meadow, the Triple Crown Connections' Summit's "Johnny-come-lately" immediately stumbled upon: his smiling peers, eleven foraging thoroughbreds, an extensive circle of white wicker peacock chairs and a brimming gourmet buffet (however because he was the overly-sentimental type, "The Master" ultimately concentrated on "catching up" with friends rather than "filling up" on free foie gras and champagne).

Now although Paradise Farms' Core Meadow was presently the site of many joyous reunions, a number of Connections were actually meeting each other for the very first time! This of course made for several fascinating conversations, like the one that was currently taking place between *Billy Turner* (Seattle Slew's trainer) and *Commander J.K.L Ross* (a Canadian Navel veteran who also happened to be the proud owner of Sir Barton). Elated that the topic of "turf history" had come up, Turner equally endeared himself to Ross when he in passing mentioned, "And there is always someone in our industry that is up in arms about how the Derby winner only gets two weeks off before the Preakness. Please! Why, Sir Barton only had ninety-six hours to catch his breath!"

Interlude - The Triple Crown Series' Conception and Maturation

While they "live" in harmony today, you could figuratively say that the Kentucky Derby and the Preakness Stakes started out as bitter rivals who hostilely vied against one other for national superiority. (This is precisely the reason why Sir Barton had just four days off in-between the "Run for the Roses" and Pimlico Race Course's premier event. Oh and incidentally, Sir Barton's Belmont Stakes triumph transpired not the traditional three weeks, but four weeks after his Preakness victory.)

So believe it or not, Sir Barton's 1919 Kentucky Derby, Preakness and Belmont sweep wasn't initially characterized a "Triple Crown" Championship. In fact, American horse racing's most regal heading really didn't even surface until the year 1930! (This was when a New York Times journalist named Bryan Field wrote about (and popularized) the "Triple Crown" that Gallant Fox had procured for Belair Stud President, William Woodward Sr.)

Now along with different gaps of space in-between each race, the Triple Crown Series has likewise seen its fair share of "longitudinal refinement". Originally stretching 1 5/8 miles when it was birthed in 1867, the Belmont Stakes was also run over: 1 1/8 miles, 1 1/4 miles and 1 3/8 miles prior to that day in 1926 when twelve furlongs (1 1/2 miles) became the norm. (Note: Sir Barton disputed the Belmont Stakes at 1 3/8 miles.) In like manner, the Preakness Stakes showcased six different distances (1 mile, 1 mile and 70 yards, 1 1/16 miles, 1 1/8 miles, 1 1/4 miles and 1 1/2 miles) before a 1 3/16 mile standard was set in 1925. Lastly, it's a little known tidbit that the Kentucky Derby was initially written as a 1 1/2 mile race when it came on the scene in 1875 (the "Run for the Roses" continued to operate under this configuration until it was permanently regressed to 1 1/4 miles in 1896).

Tragically, a few unlucky equine classes were literally denied the very opportunity to sweep Thoroughbred Horse Racing's Triple Crown Series. Why you ask? Well first off, the Kentucky Derby and the Preakness Stakes were run on the exact same day in 1917 and 1922. Similarly, the Preakness Stakes and the Belmont Stakes coincided on the calendar in 1890. Additionally, you have the fact that the Preakness Stakes wasn't even held from 1891-1893 (due to a variety of logistical complications). Moreover, the Belmont Stakes tragically "fell victim" to anti-betting legislation in both 1911 and 1912.

The reality is, only: Secretariat, Seattle Slew, Affirmed, American Pharoah and Justify have requisitioned a Triple Crown Championship under the current (and seemingly settled) format. (Gallant Fox forged his legacy during a year when the Preakness Stakes unfolded eight days before the Kentucky Derby! Omaha, War Admiral, Whirlaway, Count Fleet and Assault only had a one week sabbatical between the Kentucky Derby and Preakness Stakes. The same as Sir Barton, Citation's Preakness and Belmont conquests occurred four weeks apart.)

Even though racing fans would never see such an occurrence today, there have actually been three occasions where an eventual Triple Crown Champion was "put to use" *in-between their Preakness and Belmont starts! (Both Sir Barton and Count Fleet "tuned-up" for "The Test of a Champion" by winning Belmont Park's Withers Stakes. Comparatively, Citation ran off with Garden State Park's Jersey Stakes two weeks before he took New York by storm.)*

Seeing as how his Triple Crown Champion was a complete pushover for soft peppermints, trainer *Jimmy Jones* had thoughtfully swung by a convenience store on his way to the Connections' Summit. Soon caught up with feeding Citation's sweet tooth, the Core Meadow's "candy man" hence became startled when, from out of nowhere, a second wanting tongue appeared. Now although he was more than happy to "spread the wealth", Jones' attention was abruptly apprehended by Assault's terribly irregular right front hoof.

In back of appearing from behind the chestnut racer who'd put him on the map in 1946, jockey *Warren Mehrtens* nonchalantly pointed his index finger and then pronounced, "Imagine running across a meadow as an innocent yearling and then all of a sudden, wham! You step on a surveyor's stake!"

"It absolutely confounds me!" Jones laughed. "How can such an abnormality not disrupt this horse's action?"

Despite being hit with the same old question, Mehrtens patiently expounded, "Well as you can plainly see sir, the *"Club Footed Comet"* definitely has a walking hitch.

Yet once those gates open, it's like he totally forgets that his right front rim is bent!"

Once the initial mingling process had "faded into black", Paradise Farms' guest population kindly took their seats. It was now time to attempt the nearly impossible task of composing a Charter of Competition for Heaven's Premier Horse Race yet if nothing else, at least a spirit of democracy was in the house. (See thankfully, each and every Connection had arrived at Paradise Farms firmly believing that with regard to all matters, the majority should rule.)

After it had been established that the first order of business would be deciding exactly when Heaven's Premier Horse Race would take place, *James Fitzsimmons* (the legendary trainer who'd conditioned both Gallant Fox and Omaha for owner William Woodward Sr.) stood tall and then stressed, "Listen, nowadays these pensioners prize nap time, not digging into the final furlong of a rigorous route! What this means people, is that I'll need at least three months to prepare my racers for combat!"

As soon as the "ayes" had sanctioned Fitzsimmons' motion for a ninety-day developmental period, half of the Core Meadow's citizenry simultaneously suggested that Paradise's first ever equine fray be staged on Christmas Day. It was at this juncture that War Admiral's owner (a tremendously influential horseman named *Samuel D. Riddle*) blurted out, "I'm sorry friends, but commemorating our

Savior's birth with trivial recreation instead of devout praise and worship would be the worst kind of vanity!"

Known to all as *Ben Jones*, Whirlaway's strapping conditioner now "jumped up on his soapbox" and propositioned, "Then let's hold the race on December 31st. That gives everybody one extra week to make ready."

Ratified with booming applause, Jones' successful submission was the perfect segue into determining post time. Now of course there were some "early birds" who favored a mid-day break however these souls encountered immediate opposition from a sect who had their heart set on an evening commencement. Assault's collected owner (one *Robert J. Kleberg*) wound up pleasing everyone though when he recommended, "Simply compromise and drop the flag at 6:00 PM."

Because two rudimentary components of Heaven's Premier Horse Race were cast in stone rather quickly, there was added optimism as the conversation came in contact with the question of distance. Obviously aware that his virile Champion especially relished twelve furlongs of going, *Lucien Laurin* (Secretariat's storied conditioner) thus wasted absolutely no time interjecting, "Shouldn't Heaven's crowning thoroughbred be able to last a mere 1 1/2 miles? Come, come, all in favor say aye!"

"Uh, who told you that *Earl Sande* is a fool?!" Gallant Fox's gifted jockey cried. "Why everybody and their mother knows that "Big Red's" Belmont time is still the fastest twelve furlong dirt clocking that's ever been recorded by the hand of man! Why we'd be stupid to yield such a steep psychological advantage!"

Sensing it was the right moment to promote his own agenda, Sir Barton's trainer (the resourceful *H.G. Bedwell*) consequently submitted, "Let's not forget how far removed these horses are from actual competition! I'm telling you; if they're pushed past one mile, the possibility of injury will proliferate!"

Put off by the Core Meadow's latest charade, Affirmed's pilot resultantly proclaimed, "For those I haven't met yet, my name is *Steve Cauthen*. And now, let me be frank. I mean, I'm not saying that Mr. Bedwell doesn't esteem each Champion's physical welfare, but c'mon let's face it, the truth is, Sir Barton's chronic foot problems are well documented! Hence for him, the less distance the better. With that said, I'm of the opinion that Heaven's Premier Horse Race should unfold over our sport's traditional "classic" distance of one and a quarter miles."

(Nicknamed *"The Kid"* because he'd earned the Sport of Kings' highest honor at the tender age of eighteen, Cauthen directly obtained a supportive "Amen!" from one *Laz Barrera*.) The owner of an extra gelatinous accent, Affirmed's crafty Cuban conditioner next spiritedly added, "A ten furlong assignment is also ideal on account of it would afford a clumsy breaker sufficient time to recover!"

In that he hungered after one selfish stipulation, Samuel D. Riddle hastily forsook his champagne and then forcibly introduced, "Uh yes and since Mr. Barrera brought up the break, it seems to me that a walk up start will eliminate the peril created by one of those crude mechanical gates!"

Because it was clear what everyone was thinking, Count Fleet's jockey (the outspoken *Johnny Longden*) boisterously chuckled before he contended, "I think we all know sir that this ridiculous motion is tied to War Admiral's notorious distain for the starting gate! Well I'm sorry but a walk up start takes forever to organize and even then winds up resembling a contorted train wreck! Now as far as the contest's length is concerned, I believe that Mr. Cauthen is dead on. Yep, one and a quarter miles is the time tested measuring stick regarding route horses of this caliber!"

In back of Longden's persuasive exposition (one which helped permanently cement yet another pair of particulars) a prodigious problem relating to personnel was brought up. (See, because he had ridden both Whirlaway and Citation to a Triple Crown Championship for Calumet Farms' chief executive *Warren Wright Sr.*, Eddie Arcaro now had a decision to make.) First removing a monogrammed golf tee from his mouth, "The Master" then released, "Hey look, every single person here knows about the south Florida fishing trip that *Al Snider* never returned home from. Furthermore, I'm gonna go on record and say that, 'My good buddy would unquestionably be sitting here today had he been given the opportunity to compete in Thoroughbred Horse Racing's Triple Crown Series.' Therefore, if we do happen to hammer this thing out, then I personally think that it's our obligation to arrange a long overdue reunion between Citation and his original rider."

Though undeniably "over the top", Arcaro's exceeding generosity really came as no surprise to those who intimately knew him. Best described as an unfeigned humanitarian, thoroughbred horse racing's foremost jockey had actually split his purse winnings from the 1948 Kentucky Derby with Al Snider's widow! (Of course some theorized that "The Master" was only trying to augment his personal legacy by winning aboard Calumet's less fashionable racer however when it came time to vote, everyone (even the

Core Meadow's cynics) enthusiastically sanctioned Al Snider's instatement.)

On the heels of determining that each Champion would be assigned an impost of 126 lbs. (a no-brainer since this is the weight carried by colts throughout Thoroughbred Horse Racing's Triple Crown Series), *Karen Taylor* (Seattle Slew's co-owner along with her husband *Mickey*) matter-of-factly squeezed in, "You know I hate to rain on everyone's parade but I've been sitting here for the last half hour thinking, *'Um, so like where exactly is this race supposed to take place?'*"

Whereas he was on the same page as the Summit's latest speaker, *Don Cameron* (Count Fleet's conditioner) scooted forward in his seat and then added, "That is my question exactly! I mean only God is familiar with the totality of *His* Paradise however to the best of my knowledge, there aren't any thoroughbred racetracks up here!"

Someone who often thought out loud, *Penny Chenery* (Secretariat's cultivated owner) as a result daydreamed, "Mm, wouldn't it be great if we could just ship our Champions to Churchill Downs and be done with it?"

As he pointed towards the ground, Samuel D. Riddle quipped, "Yeah well Churchill Downs is down there and we're up here ma'am! Besides, even if such a scheme were possible, all of Horse Racing Nation automatically associates Churchill Downs with the Kentucky Derby! The point I'm trying to make is; this engagement needs its own identity."

Ultimately cutting her second sentence short (because everyone's eyes had begun to wander), Penny Chenery next sat is a state of puzzlement until she too surveyed the long winding bejeweled cobblestone

16

thoroughfare that connected Paradise Farms' parking lot and the Core Meadow. (Measuring over eighteen hands, the fossil grey Percheron who had abruptly breezed in was now actually only about a stone's throw away from crashing the party!) Presently in the process of transporting two cavaliers, the Core Meadow's largest equine did so courtesy of a cherry wood Coupé Carriage that was enriched with: white onyx accents, 24kt gold mezzotint and solid platinum wheel spokes.

Consistent with the ride they had pulled up in, Paradise Farms' enigmatic trespassers truly reeked of quality. (Comprehensively dressed in their "Sunday best", stranger A&B in fact both brandished: black Vicuña wool overcoats, satin collapsible top hats and crocodile skin dress shoes.) Subsequent to disembarking double-quick and courteously removing his chapeau, the soul who'd been traveling "shotgun" ceremoniously said, "Honorary Connections of Heaven's Triple Crown Champions, please allow me to introduce myself! My name is *August Belmont*, and I now beg your forgiveness for this impertinent intrusion! Assuredly, we have no intent of levying chaos! On the contrary, my business partner and I only have your absolute best interests at heart!"

One of those who grasped the present situation's gravity, William Woodward Sr. thus leaped from his chair while he exclaimed, "My goodness, the very soul the Belmont Stakes is named after!"

In an effort to erase the befuddlement from Karen Taylor's face, H.G. Bedwell leaned over and whispered, "Belmont was a prominent political figure in New York throughout the mid 1800's however his real passion is highborn horseflesh. Believe you me lassie, that hombre

17

labored tirelessly to help lay the very foundation that American thoroughbred racing is built on."

Once he'd rolled up the reigns, Paradise Farm's other gate-crasher touched down and declared, "Salutations friends! *Leonard Walter Jerome* here! Now, on top of seconding Mr. Belmont's apology, I want to likewise assure that we only seek to be your humble servants!"

The result of being star struck twice over, William Woodward Sr. impulsively gasped, "Holy smokes; it's the *"King of Wall Street"*!"

Consequent to seeing Karen Taylor disconcertedly look his way, H.G. Bedwell freshly summarized, "Uh, Mr. Jerome belongs on "Thoroughbred Racing's Mount Rushmore" as well ma'am. Not to mention, that there chap was also a flamboyant financier who won and lost incredible monetary fortunes via the New York Stock Exchange."

As he delightedly raced forward to receive Paradise Farms' patriarchs, William Woodward Sr. euphorically emit, "Well we obviously didn't expect to be graced by two of our industry's founding fathers however on behalf of everyone here, I bestow a warm welcome gentlemen! It is indeed our own selves who are your servants!"

While still locked in a firm handshake with Gallant Fox's and Omaha's owner, Leonard Jerome replied, "Much obliged sir much obliged! And at this time friends, I'd like to reveal the reason behind this surprise visitation!"

Although unexpectedly hit with a request to "tarry for a few", Leonard Jerome and August Belmont both submissively silenced themselves as Ariel supplied some more refreshments and an additional pair of white wicker peacock chairs. Soon saying "thank you" for his gratuitous dose of dry champagne, Jerome next "wet his beak" and then continued with, "Well, like I was saying, we've dropped by because when word concerning this Summit reached my estate, I immediately turned to my business partner and said, 'August, I might know of a place where they can stage Heaven's Premier Horse Race!'"

"I knew it!" William Woodward Sr. hollered. "I knew in the excessive enormousness of Heaven, there had to be a racetrack somewhere!"

Through a broad smile, the "King of Wall Street" related, "And assuredly sir, I'm not here to tell you about just any oval! You see the Belmont Stakes, a.k.a., the eldest leg of Thoroughbred Horse Racing's Triple Crown Series, was inaugurated at Jerome Park Racetrack in 1867! Come now friends, I mean, what locale could be more fitting for a contest that is to feature Heaven's eleven Triple Crown Champions?!"

Thrown for a loop like everyone else, William Woodward Sr. thus cross-examined, "Uh, did you say Jerome Park? As in the racetrack that was demolished in 1894 to make way for an official New York City water reservoir? Pardon me sir but how can a defunct hippodrome, an Earthly one at that, possibly aid our cause?"

Once he had given himself adequate time to recall every word from a carefully rehearsed dissertation, Jerome gently rose up and recited, "Esteemed Connections; please bear with me as I rewind to the beginning of a long and sorted adventure. See, even though my Earthly plentitude satisfied to an extent, there had always been a divine dream written across my heart, one which involved constructing New York's, and for that matter, North America's preeminent thoroughbred racetrack. Mm, believe me when I say that inside of nightly apparitions her flawless

19

embodiment appeared to me: picturesque, wild and romantic, like New Market in America. Now inherently, I knew that securing my course's proper mold meant talking to one Charles Wheatly, a feverish thoroughbred enthusiast and designer of the old Saratoga Race Course."

Savvy he'd secured his audience's interest, the "King of Wall Street" therefore pumped up his vocal volume before he persisted with, "Months into a sustained search for the perfect land plot, Wheatly and I inspected *James Bathgate's* two hundred and thirty acre Westchester estate. Granted, because it would cost thousands to level the hills that swathed this district, Charles immediately advised me to "keep looking". However after thinking long and hard about it, I came to the conclusion that these rolling rises would actually supply my infield with uncommon character!"

"You have got some initiative!" Jimmy Jones acknowledged. "Erecting a full scale thoroughbred racetrack is an astronomic undertaking!"

After he'd heartily agreed with Jones' sentiment, August Belmont advertised, "And make no mistake folks; Mr. Jerome's ambition was not solely limited to just fashioning his "dream oval"! You see, my business partner also conceptualized and founded the "American Jockey Club"; i.e., a board of trustees responsible for meticulously cultivating every single solitary aspect of Jerome Park. Of course, these accredited horsemen bequeathed quite the honor when they elected yours truly as their inaugural President!"

"Please don't take offense, but it sounds so distant in a way." Karen Taylor remarked. "You know, that era in which you gentlemen operated."

In an effort to bridge a broad generational gap, Jerome eagerly elaborated, "Try and picture it ma'am. The year was 1866 and beneath an electric blue September sky, Jerome Park commenced a four day meet distinctive to anything previously seen in American racing circles. Scattered across my rolling infield were dozens of high-wrought horse drawn carriages, each saturated with colorful patrons who exuded savoir fare. Amid the sounds of a symphony orchestra, gorgeous damsels distributed vouchers which were good for the Clubhouse's complimentary gourmet brunch buffet. Jam-packed by post time, the Main Grandstand literally shook beneath those shouts that were aimed at the starter's hoisted flag. Subsequently, a cordon bleu card gorged with impeccable equine talent was initiated. Of course, the evenings that accompanied this christening were vivacious, so much so that the lanterns overhanging my Clubhouse's porch burned well into the wee hours. It was truly an age of distinct ambiance, and in the words of one newspaper columnist, 'A sui generis thoroughbred racing bazaar which will never be exceeded!'"

"Why the premature demise then?" Steve Cauthen pried. "What I'm saying is; how does a water reservoir of all things supplant an incomparable thoroughbred racing complex?!"

As the life drained from his eyes, the "King of Wall Street" morosely sighed, "Ironically enough, Jerome Park was undone by, well, gambling if you can believe it."

While making a face that showed he was clearly taken aback, "The Kid" maintained, "C'mon, wagering is to horse racing like peanut butter is to jelly! How then could our industry's very lifeblood sabotage your venue?"

In back of promising an eventual explanation, Jerome reflected, "From its grand opening on, my racetrack handled what could only be described as colossal sums of capital. Admittedly, our auction pools regularly exceeded five thousand dollars and before you scoff, please realize that in 1866, most Americans earned less than one dollar per day. Our economy was so gilded in fact that a pool inferior to five hundred bucks was genuinely considered a bagatelle that was hardly worth selling!"

Following a much longed for reconciliation with his champagne, the "King of Wall Street" tacked on, "Truth be told though friends, everything didn't revolve around betting when I first opened shop. I mean believe it or not, both owners and punters alike earnestly coveted the thrill of victory over boosting their bankrolls! However, rather than a lack of lasciviousness, do you know what I miss most about those early days? I miss how the vanquished would without fail, make it a point to walk over and sincerely congratulate those who had won the day!"

Since he had always worked hard to weave sportsmanship into the fabric of Calumet Farms' culture, Warren Wright Sr. supportively boomed, "Here, here! You know, and I'm a firm believer that, 'Only in defeat can one show what they are truly made of.'"

Once the applause whipped up by Wright's comment had ceased, the Connections' Summit's key note speaker further rambled, "That sir, is actually August Belmont's favorite saying! Ha, that's probably because he is equal parts meekness and munificence! And uh, speaking of charity, I'd like to mention that though my business partner collected no salary during his Presidential tenure, he nonetheless committed three hundred and sixty-five days of every year to the American Jockey Club's aforementioned creed!"

Less patient than William Woodward Sr. (who was still waiting for an answer to his own question), Steve Cauthen hence inserted, "And I think it's fairly obvious that you decided to institute the "Belmont Stakes" as a means to honor your business partner's undying dedication! I'm still wondering though sir how gambling of all things dissolved your empire!"

Subsequent to voicing an apology for his drawn out digression, Jerome recounted, "Over the course of time, both bookmakers and pari-mutuel machines permeated our sport's landscape. Convenient betting outlets meant an explosion in clientele however unfortunately, many of these fledglings peddled corruption. Rumors soon swirled that several riders had been bribed to "hold their horses back" yet even more despicable were those whispers which alleged how some barns were actually purchasing and administering illegal "performance enhancing equine meds". Well, my stress level ultimately became such that I seriously pondered closing up shop but right then came the controversial United States presidential election of 1876. See, because mass violence continued to erupt between those who had bet on either *Samuel J. Tilden* or *Rutherford B. Hayes*, all these new anti-betting laws suddenly started sweeping the land!"

Finally inspired to join the conversation, *Johnny Loftus* (Sir Barton's hard boiled jockey) first popped half a strawberry in his mouth and then drawled, "Mm, so basically what you're saying is, the "powers that be" kinda made your decision for you."

Weary of watching his best friend unstitch an old wound, Belmont on that account concluded, "Though essentially stripped of its bread and butter, Jerome Park managed to retain a faint pulse because a couple of regional guilds still needed a location where they could exercise their horses. In time however, the "Suburban Riding and Driving Club" methodically lured these boosters away. Thankfully mind you, I can also mention that both Leonard and I were "called home" before Jerome Park was appropriated and callously leveled."

"Well I guess that brings us right back to square one." William Woodward Sr. indicated. "Therefore I'll respectfully ask again. How can a defunct hippodrome, an Earthly one at that, possibly aid our cause?"

Though aware that an ambiguous answer might not be appreciated at this point, Jerome nevertheless tooted, "God's grace with regards to Thoroughbred Horse Racing's Triple Crown Series far transcends this meadow's equine population sir!"

Following a five second pause wherein he connected the dots, Woodward shockingly inquired, "Wait a minute?! Are you saying that when they "die" every racetrack tied to Thoroughbred Horse Racing's Triple Crown Series "goes to Heaven"?!"

"That's one way of putting it." Jerome laughed. "Yep, for whatever reason, the *Ancient of Days* definitely has a soft spot for the "Sport of Kings"!"

As astonished mouths dropped all around him, H.G. Bedwell spieled, "New York's Morris Park Race Course hosted the Preakness Stakes in 1890 and the Belmont Stakes from 1890 to 1904. Correspondingly, Gravesend Racetrack in Coney Island accommodated the Preakness Stakes from 1894 to 1908. What that means folks, is that these two ovals are also up here somewhere!"

"I met a retired groom once who had worked at Morris Park Race Course." Jimmy Jones wistfully inputted. "He always used to say, 'Jimmy my boy, Morris was the "cat's meow"!'"

Understandably terrified that H.G. Bedwell and Jimmy Jones had opened up a huge "can of worms", the "King of Wall Street" thus jumped in and marketed, "Look, Morris and Gravesend are no doubt fabulous facilities and to be honest, I am good friends with the men who built these theaters. However, did either complex originate the most primeval leg of Thoroughbred Horse Racing's Triple Crown Series!?"

"Noted are Jerome Park's ties to the Belmont Stakes sir." Mickey Taylor articulated. "However when it comes down to employing a venue, I'm of the mind that merit supersedes nostalgia. Therefore, I motion that we delay finalizing the Charter of Competition until every available oval can be put under a microscope."

Angry with what had entered his ears, Laz Barrera for that reason argued, "Why are we looking a gift horse in the mouth people?! I mean, these gentlemen are handing us the birthplace of Thoroughbred Horse Racing's Triple Crown Series on a silver platter!"

"But do we really want to ship sight unseen?" Ben Jones concernedly asked. "You know, I for one believe that Mr. Taylor has the right idea! We should go corporately inspect: Jerome Park, Morris Park and this here Gravesend Racetrack, and then make our decision."

Stepping in anew with hopes of saving the Connections a lot of time and trouble, Samuel D. Riddle begged for order and then broadcasted, "Ladies and gentlemen, over the course of a highly indulgent eighty-nine year lifespan, these eyes beheld nearly every acceptable thoroughbred racetrack the world over. A few were worth "writing home about" yet before I "crossed over" I took the trouble to journalize, '*My closest brush with equine utopia occurred inside of a long gone amphitheater, one that briefly graced James Bathgate's former estate.*' Uh, in other words people, seeing as how the terrestrial version of Jerome Park was literally "Heaven on Earth", well then I highly doubt that the eternal version of this racetrack will eh, disappoint you."

Falling into full agreement with War Admiral's owner this time around, Johnny Longden resultantly spouted, "Man I'm willing to take a leap of faith! Besides, who knows if the owners of Morris and Gravesend even have a heart to host this affair?! Anyway, here's the bottom line folks, we should just put this thing to a vote and be done with it!"

"I second the motion!" Riddle harmoniously roared. "All in favor of staging Heaven's Premier Horse Race at Jerome Park Racetrack say aye!"

Although he ended up pulling away from Paradise Farms without his "dream result" (i.e., a landslide victory), Leonard Jerome nevertheless knew that a win was a win. Placing his mouth on hold until the Core Meadow was some fifteen hundred yards back, the "King of Wall Street" finally sighed, "Well we did it August, albeit only by three votes."

"Acquisitioning a bit more of the majority certainly would have made life easier." Belmont bemoaned. "As it stands, we're going to grow mighty weary of accepting tearful apologies."

Charitably acting as the Connections' Summit's assigned scribe, Penny Chenery was exactly four letters into writing out the official "Charter of Competition" for Heaven's Premier Horse Race when *Max Hirsch* (Assault's leathery conditioner) infringed, "Hang on a second ma'am, I just had a thought. Now, I think we all came into this Summit with an understanding that we wouldn't be competing for a "purse" per se, however, I do think that the winning Connections should leave Jerome Park with some kind of trophy!"

Having earned the sobriquet of *"Smokey"* because he was seldom seen without a cigar, *Willie Saunders* (a.k.a., Omaha's jockey) made good use of his portable ashtray before he blazoned, "Man I have a better idea! For once, let's give the winning horse a trophy instead! Hey, how about a prize that includes a strand from each Champion's mane?! That is, if you owners don't mind seeing your fur-babies donate a lock or two."

In the wake of "making it unanimous", Samuel D. Riddle slapped on, "You know and given his appearance, I would bet that Mr. Jerome knows an artisan who is capable of manufacturing the perfect memento!"

Disinclined to stall her pen again, Penny Chenery thus kept her head down as she hearkened unto yet another "eleventh hour" proposal. Submitted by Karen Taylor and promptly converted into law courtesy of a ninety-five percent majority, the final article pinned to the Charter of Competition plainly read, *"All participating Connections are strictly prohibited from placing either public or private wagers on Heaven's Premier Horse Race."*

After it was universally autographed and sent through Paradise Farms' Xerox machine (so that every Connection could retain a copy), the official Charter of Competition for Heaven's Premier Horse Race was securely mailed to the address that was printed on Leonard Jerome's platinum foil business card.

Ultimately answering a 6:00 PM knock from an angel who worked for "Cherub Couriers Inc.", the "King of Wall Street" subsequently signed for his special delivery package while he appealed, "If you please August, pick up the phone and call the "Eternity Times'" breaking news hotline. Those scribes will be interested to know that thoroughbred horse racing will soon make its long awaited debut inside the Kingdom of Heaven!"

29

Chapter 2 - The First Shippers

Currently cruising through the dawn at 30 m.p.h. (compliments of H. G. Bedwell's 1969 Buick Skylark), Commander J.K.L Ross now took in the lighted billboard that read, "Welcome to Paradise Farms" as he leadenly told, "Thanks for driving Harvey, I've still only got one eye open."

Donning his usual brown wool suit and black derby, Sir Barton's spindly conditioner first switched on his turn signal before he restlessly replied, "I'm right there with you sir. However there's not a moment to lose if we really expect to resurrect a long retired racehorse in just fourteen weeks!"

Since his acting chauffeur was already showing signs of being totally stressed, Ross went to counseling, "Deep breaths Harvey, deep breaths. Dear me, at this rate you'll be on blood pressure medication by week's end."

Interlude - Sir Barton, the "Sport of Kings'" Improbable Immortal

Despite being purchased by Commander J.K.L Ross in 1918 for $10,000 (these days that's approximately $150,000!), thoroughbred racing's primordial imperator was hardly a child prodigy. On the contrary, Sir Barton didn't even manage to "hit the board" (finish 1st, 2nd or 3rd) until the sixth and final start of his sophomore campaign. (Granted, this was a game second place effort in Belmont Park's famed Futurity Stakes.)

Now on New Year's Day in 1919, Commander J.K.L. Ross passionately resolved to win the forthcoming Kentucky Derby with his beloved equine star, Billy Kelly. On paper at least, Billy Kelly's primary nemesis was a horse named Eternal and since this one dimensional racer habitually seized command early, Bedwell and Ross resourcefully reached into their bottomless bag of tricks. Hare-footed in his own right, Sir Barton was therefore entered into the "Run for the Roses" with the ulterior motive of luring Eternal into a suicidal speed duel, one which would (in theory) "set up" the late closing Billy Kelly.

In accordance with Bedwell's and Ross' strategy, Johnny Loftus immediately opened up on his eleven Derby foes once the flag fell however it was soon evident that Eternal didn't much like Churchill Downs' "muddy going". Alas, the day's theoretic breakneck pace never developed. Instead, Sir Barton scored by five lengths in wire to wire fashion over Billy Kelly (who still closed gamely for second despite an unfavorable trip). As for Eternal's fate, well, to the dismay of many punters who'd gone "all-in", the post-time favorite wound up staggering home in tenth position, beaten some thirty lengths.

Although he was initially tagged a "one hit wonder" who'd been excessively aided by an "off track", Sir Barton was just getting started. Back in action just four days after leaving Louisville (this time over a lightning "fast" strip), Commander J.K.L. Ross' crotchety upstart went on to silence his many naysayers by outrunning an accomplished Preakness field (one which included Eternal) by four lengths.

31

Ultimately exiting Baltimore as thoroughbred racing's most popular equine, Sir Barton subsequently punched his ticket to Paradise Farms at the expense of two hopelessly overmatched Belmont rivals.

Off the pace of parallel parking in behind Paradise Farms' gold overlaid Primary Barn, H.G. Bedwell promptly escorted Commander J.K.L Ross down to Sir Barton's gaudy abode. Now though usually unflappable, Ross proceeded to "melt down" when he discovered that stall #1's resident equine was "missing in action". Thankfully before the Marines were called in, Bedwell obeyed his intuition and then cried out, "Over here sir!"

Just around the corner, one *Toots Thompson* was attentively administering Sir Barton's morning field bath and as he locked eyes with his Champion's radically devoted groom, Commander J.K.L. Ross stanchly declared, "You're a horse whisperer if ever there was one Toots. Yes sir! Why the cherub who cleans this stall told me that he typically can't get within ten feet of him!"

While he cheerfully wiped down his "master's" withers, Thompson made plain, "I ain't no horse whisperer sir. It's just that for whatever reason, I'm the only living thing this here animal doesn't hate."

"If I walked around on those feet all day, I'd be in a bad mood too." Bedwell lamented. "Oy-vey, one Achilles' heel is headache enough, lucky us though, we get four times the fun."

One who was all too familiar with Sir Barton's especially soft and thus habitually sore hooves, Commander J.K.L. Ross now openly admitted, "You know all through the Summit I was reflecting on what an utter complexity it is to shoe this cantankerous animal. Ha, hey Harvey, remember the time you tried to pad his feet by gluing piano felt to the tops of his shoes?"

Hardly in the mood to skip down memory lane, Bedwell nevertheless cited, "The only reason that scheme didn't work was because it required "normal size" ferrier nails due to all the extra layering. Of course we all know that this fella can only tolerate a pint sized spike, hence the reason why he throws more shoes than a mob of political protestors. Yep, only horse I ever saw return from a race completely barefoot!"

As he wrung a quart of soapy water out of his trusty orange sponge, Thompson encouraged, "Ah it may take some improvising, but we'll get him up and running. Say boss, you gonna ship today?"

Subsequent to tearing his eyes off of Sir Barton's delicate tootsies, Commander J.K.L. Ross' top assistant acknowledged, "Yes, with only a three month window there's no time to waste! Plus, I secured us an early morning appointment tomorrow with Mr. Jerome's ferrier. Mm, *Bishop* is his name, *Ethan Bishop*. Supposedly, there's never been a horse this guy couldn't shoe."

"Well, I'll be finished up with his biggest challenge to date in just a few minutes boss." Thompson smilingly filled in. "What then?"

33

Because Sir Barton had suddenly decided to shake off some excess bath water, Bedwell wound up spitting out a load of soap suds while he summarized, "You know that massive equine motor coach out in the parking lot that is labeled, '**Property of Paradise Farms**'? Well, you can load our gear into the back of it because Ariel is going to drive you both over to the local train depot at eleven o'clock. From there you'll board the high-noon express to Jerome Park. Eh, it's about a two and a half hour ride but don't sweat it, the Commander here sprung for a deluxe rail car, it comes with a private chef and everything! Hey and Jerome's people know that you're coming so they'll be waiting to help you get settled in. After that just relax but keep your phone handy, I'll touch base around suppertime."

Following a few more minutes of "shop talk", H.G. Bedwell and Commander J.K.L Ross put an eye on both their ride and the nearest corner store (a.k.a., that place where they could grab some coffee). Siphoning through a thousand thoughts as he walked, Sir Barton's drowsy owner as a result wound up mentioning, "Oh hey and don't forget, we need to find out if Jerome owns a few sparring partners that we can utilize."

"If not, I'll just call around to some local farms and round up a few." Bedwell certified. "Huh, it's crazy isn't it? I mean, how your boy simply refuses to breeze with any real enthusiasm unless he's in company with another beast."

In back of admitting that his racer was definitely one of a kind, Ross dictated, "Say now that I think about it Harvey, why don't you get on the horn and tell Loftus to get over here. You know, just in case Toots needs an extra pair of hands on the ride over."

34

Even though morning rush hour had arrayed him with ten white knuckles, Johnny Loftus slowly recaptured his serenity as he watched Toots Thompson braid Sir Barton's bristling mane. Alas, Loftus' peace was pilfered once again when a voice from the distant past pestered, "Well, looks like he's standing o.k. today. Question is, will those feet hold up over the long haul?"

As he resisted an acute temptation to turn around, Paradise Farms' provoked jockey countered, "Why don't you go bother someone else, like the twelve hundred pound sloth that lives next door. Before you scat however, I'll wager a sawbuck against your fiver that Gallant Fox isn't even awake yet!"

In back of lining up beside his biggest rival and longtime friend, Earl Sande chattered, "Why in the world would I bet against a dead certainty? Ha, and since you brought it up, you'll get a kick out of this one brother! So the boss man is sending the four of us over on the 4:00 PM train rather than the high-noon express for the sole reason that my guy likes to sleep in until lunchtime! I swear, sometimes I wonder who is in charge of our outfit, Woodward or the *"Fox of Belair"*?! Aside from all that though I must say, Ross' lad hasn't aged a bit! Incredible! I mean he still looks like the same horse that I rode in the Belmont Futurity! Uh, remind me again why I jumped ship on the first Saturday in May?"

While he continued to laugh, Loftus reproached, "Because like an egg-head, you let Ross convince you that Billy Kelly couldn't lose."

Amid absorbing the salt that had been rubbed into his ancient wound, Sande achingly alleged, "Yeah well, should've, would've, could've. And yes, I should have four Kentucky Derby titles instead of three however all and all, I think it's safe to say that we both ultimately "rode off into the sunset" with no regrets."

"Uh, speak for yourself there buddy!" Loftus howled. "Lest you forget, August 13th, 1919, the day yours truly came home second in the Sanford Memorial Stakes. Dude, Riddle is still icy towards me on account of that result!"

Forever looking at the bright side of things, Gallant Fox's captain thus consoled, "Why that's ridiculous! What about all the times you landed *Man o' War* in the winner's circle for that guy?! It's something like seven isn't it?"

"Eight, eight times." stall #1's scapegoat bitterly grumbled. "But believe me Earl; Riddle only remembers that Man o' War's lone defeat from twenty-one career starts occurred while I was in the driver's seat."

Spieling as if he was in the pulpit, Sande now sermonized, "Every jockey goes through the valley Johnny. And if you'll pardon the cliché, I do believe that, 'Our trials only make us stronger!'"

In the course of putting an eye on his Champion's "problem area", Loftus sighed, "Stronger huh? Well I hope you're right man 'cause it's gonna take some serious muscle to pilot a horse with four bald tires past this field!"

As he continued to wait beneath the three story Juniper tree which helped lend shade to Paradise Farms' Primary Barn, Eddie Arcaro intermittently peered over at the little squirt that lived four doors down from Sir Barton. Now although his backside was perpetually kissed by fans and horsemen alike, "The Master" never ever received even a sliver of acknowledgement from the thoroughbred that had essentially made him a household name. However rather than stew over how Whirlaway always "looked right through him", Arcaro purposefully placed his focus on the plethora of good things that were wrapped up inside of stall #5's "small package".

Interlude - A Horse of a Different Color

Though blessed with a brilliant chestnut coat, Whirlaway's defining physical characteristic was his exceptionally long tail. Resembling a "fifth leg", the aforementioned appendage likewise lengthened Warren Wright Sr.'s eccentric racer by five whole feet whenever he was in full flight. Consequently, Horse Racing Nation reasonably christened Calumet Farms' first eventual immortal (what else but) "Mr. Longtail".

Much as he was "out in left field", Eddie Arcaro's chosen mount sure enough owned an almost mythical closing kick. Oftentimes however, Whirlaway would severely compromise his chances by "bolting" wide when the gates opened. Despite this damaging attribute, Warren Wright Sr.'s "hoofed head case" won handily at first asking (even though he ran every single step of his debut up against the outer rail).

In no way bullet proof, Whirlaway did in fact cost himself the 1941 Bluegrass Stakes by virtue of plotting a ridiculously wide course. (A logical fall guy, then jockey Wendall Eads absorbed an abundance of criticism for his failure to bridal the nation's number one Kentucky Derby prospect. In like manner, Eads came under fire yet again when "Mr. Longtail" lost the Derby Trial as a result of badly "blowing" Churchill Downs' far turn.)

Fearful that favorable expectations for the "Run for the Roses" were gradually slipping away, Ben Jones hence implemented a major strategic overhaul. So along with enlisting Eddie Arcaro, Jones also began taking his problem child for lengthy walks directly aside Churchill Downs' inner rail. Eventually questioned about these sustained strolls by one Warren Wright Sr., Calumet's senior conditioner in turn responded, "It's a simple adaptation scheme sir. See, the more he hangs out down along the wood, the more likely it is that he'll want to race down along the wood."

Ultimately carrying out one last stratagem right in the paddock on Derby Day, Ben Jones went ahead and used his pocket knife to amputate Whirlaway's left "blinker". (Blinkers - Typically consisting of plastic cups that are attached to a cloth hood, this piece of equipment augments concentration by reducing a horse's field of vision.) A trick *he'd picked up while conditioning harness racers, Jones assured Eddie Arcaro that liberating "Mr. Longtail's" left eye would only further persuade him to spy the rail and thus, pursue a ground saving trip. Initially skeptical, "The Master" nevertheless sang his superior's praises as he approached the finish line eight lengths in front.*

In that exact moment where he thought, *"Maybe I should call him,"* Eddie Arcaro heard a commotion erupt behind stall #1. Soon taking off for a stroll around the corner, "The Master" next permitted Al Snider to bequeath his "John Hancock" a few more times before he jested, "Oh, I see how it is, you put me on hold so that you can stand here and sign autographs!"

As he turned his attention away from the band of Guardian Angels that had surrounded him, thoroughbred racing's "prodigal son" announced, "There he is folks, there's the reason why I'm not still down at the lake fishing for blue gill!"

In an attempt to downplay his friend's flattery, "The Master" digressed, "O.K., let's not get carried away Al. Like I said on the phone, everyone who attended the Summit had a hand in this as well. Anyway, let's hit the road, brunch is on me."

While he took back his autograph book, Citation's assigned cherub chirped, "Sakes alive, first you get the winning horse, and now a free meal. Shucks Mr. Snider, it must be your lucky week!"

Cognizant that the commenced mass debate which centered on who would win Heaven's Premier Horse Race was destined to boil over, Arcaro for that reason urged, "C'mon Al let's roll, there's a Belgium Waffle across the street with your name on it."

To say the least, Laz Barrera's mid-day meeting with *Louis Wolfson* had gotten off to a rocky start. See, even though he was in company with Affirmed's no-nonsense owner right outside of stall #11, Barrera couldn't help but reverentially gawk at the "Big Red" horse that was foraging in the middle of Paradise Farms' Core Meadow. Finally fed up with playing second fiddle, Wolfson therefore kicked the Primary Barn's eleventh support pillar ahead of snarling, "You know if you're scared of him Laz, then we might as well just stay home!"

Subsequent to redirecting his sightline, Barrera respectfully contrasted, "Remember the fight *Alydar* put up sir? Well I'm just bracing myself for all that times ten!"

Interlude - Affirmed vs. Alydar

The fiercest rivalry that has ever "spilt over" into Thoroughbred Horse Racing's Triple Crown Series, Affirmed and Alydar first slugged it out as sophomores at Belmont Park on June 15, 1977. That day the Youthful Stakes went to Affirmed however Alydar evened the ledger three weeks later by capturing Belmont Park's Great American Stakes. The struggle next shifted to Saratoga Race Course where a fresh face named Steve Cauthen landed Affirmed on the favorable side of a half length decision in the Hopeful Stakes.

Compelled to "mix things up" after he was spoon fed another close defeat in Belmont Park's Futurity Stakes, John Veitch (Alydar's cagey conditioner) accordingly went ahead and enlisted jockey Jorge Velásquez. A future hall of famer, Velásquez and his new sidekick subsequently beat Laz Barrera's "equine bulldozer" in Belmont Park's 107th Champagne Stakes. Not far downstream, round six saw Affirmed narrowly steal the Laurel Futurity, an accomplishment which earned Louis Wolfson's blue-chip "Two-Year Old Championship" honors.

Following a restful winter, Affirmed warmed up for the 1978 Triple Crown Series by bagging: Santa Anita Park's San Felipe Stakes, Santa Anita Park's Santa Anita Derby and Hollywood Park's Hollywood Derby. Following suit back east, John Veitch's invaluable racer raided: Hialeah Park's Flamingo Stakes, Gulfstream Park's Florida Derby and Keenland Race Course's Bluegrass Stakes. Conclusively sent off as the 6/5 favorite in the 104th Kentucky Derby, Alydar's initial poky traction ultimately set him back a country mile and although an unbelievable rally made things interesting,

Affirmed wound up reining beneath the Twin Spires by 1 1/2 lengths.

In the aftermath of Affirmed's super slim Preakness win over Alydar, an exasperated John Veitch went back to the drawing board. Conclusively commanded to, "Go for the jugular," Jorge Velásquez hence threw down the gauntlet as he exited Belmont Park's first turn (yet the idea of an eight furlong match race certainly didn't scare Steve Cauthen). Now along with being precariously pinned down on the rail every step of the way, Louis Wolfson's royal aspirant was also headed in the lane however inside of that moment where "The Kid" boldly plied a previously untested left handed whip, Affirmed gustily scraped together the exact amount of will needed to procure a "nostril sized" score.

Suddenly in an even worse mood (because he had scuffed up his brand new Italian leather loafers), Louis Wolfson consequently squawked, "Uh, can we please just worry about our own horse here Laz?! Now, do you think that we're better off shipping by truck or by rail?"

"I mean there are pros and cons either way sir." Barrera puffed. "But since Cauthen knows your animal best, I think that we should get his opinion before we cement anything."

As he peeked over his shoulder at stall #11's interior wall clock, Wolfson growled, "Oh we will, that is, if he ever decides to grace us with his presence! Ugh, look man, I have to go borrow Ariel's bathroom. You hang here and keep a lookout."

In the aftermath of being abandoned, Barrera proceeded to lovingly pet his Champion's majestic muzzle (however just as things started to get real "mushy", Steve Cauthen barreled around the corner). Nearly scared out of his shoes, Affirmed's conditioner thus clutched his chest before he indignantly said, "Son, you know the boss is a stickler when it comes to punctuality; what gives?!"

Amid catching his breath, "The Kid" embarrassingly explained, "Shoot, I'm sorry Laz. I was ordering a new exercise saddle online and lost track of time. Wolfson didn't leave did he?"

"No, he went to use the bathroom." Barrera sighed. "Anyway look, we were talking logistics before you got here and since you know Affirmed best, do you think that we're better off shipping by truck or by rail?"

Baited by the sight of Seattle Slew's noggin sticking out from stall #10, Cauthen resultantly ranted, "You know I've never gotten over it Laz, the way '78 ended for us I mean. Yup, Woodbine Racetrack's inaugural Marlboro Cup and Belmont Park's 60th Jockey Club Gold Cup. We're talking the only two races in history that featured a pair of Triple Crown Champions and both times that rascal there outperformed us. O.K., I can admit that we just weren't good enough up in Canada but I'm telling you, we would've gotten square in New York if my saddle hadn't of slipped!"

While he pursed his lips, Affirmed's trainer unsympathetically mocked, "*My saddle slipped, my saddle slipped!* Man if I've heard it once I've heard it a thousand times! Just let it go finally will you?! Gracious sakes, Slew got nosed at the wire in the Gold Cup by *Exeller* anyway so what does it matter? Now listen to me son, if all you have on the brain is some nonsensical vendetta, you're gonna lose sight of the big picture. Uh, like the fact that we're pursuing the most transcendent title in our sport's history!"

Rolling in just as Barrera letup, Louis Wolfson went on to add, "Yes we are, and therefore a jockey who owns a watch is at the top of my wish list! Oh and speaking of time Laz, I want you here at 6:00 AM tomorrow morning with that goose neck horse trailer of yours. Cauthen, you'll help us pack and then climb in back for the ride over. Got it?!"

Though disappointed what had started off as a democracy had suddenly become a dictatorship, "The Kid" nevertheless smilingly submitted, "I'll be here sir, uh, and with much time to spare!"

Accessing the Primary Barn's seventh stall at approximately 1:46 PM with a brimming wheel barrel, Max Hirsch subsequently offloaded a 100 lb. plastic bag that was labeled, "Shadrach's Supplemental Organic Equine Vittles". Quick to top-off Assault's sterling silver oat trough, Hirsch next opened his smart phone's internet browser (however before the upcoming week's weather forecast could completely download, three rambunctious neighs rang out). See, the "Club Footed Comet" had basically made like an industrial vacuum cleaner and was now (in horsey language) spiritedly saying, "Uh, seconds please!"

As he compliantly conferred "course #2", Max Hirsch sentimentally conjured up his very first memory of stall #7's four-legged gorger. Having been called out to Robert J. Kleberg's magnificent Texas based King Ranch, Hirsch amusedly took in Assault's walking hitch for a few minutes and then howled, "Make a racehorse out of him?! Please Bob, why that lemon couldn't outrun your wife's Shetland pony!"

Interlude - The Lone Star State's Equine Heavyweight

A horse who initially struggled to "connect the dots", Assault in fact began his lengthy six year forty-two race career by going a dismal "two for nine". Now in back of kicking off 1946 with a minor stakes win, the "Club Footed Comet" spectacularly (and surprisingly) appropriated Aqueduct Racetrack's prestigious Wood Memorial. Even so, an ensuing fourth place finish in the Derby Trial drove away virtually every fair weather fan. A stand up guy if ever there was one, Max Hirsch immediately tried to take the heat off of his beaten racer by publicly stating, "The mud boots I put him in were too gaping for that sloppy of a strip. Why they were spilling over with sludge by the five-eighths pole. Heck, he would've had an easier time pulling an engine block around the oval!"

Ultimately romping home by eight lengths as the fourth pari-mutuel choice in the Kentucky Derby, Assault in turn rewarded his loyalists with a whopping $18.40 "Win Mutual" (this "price" is based on a $2 wager). "Rushed" to the lead following a botched break, the "Club Footed Comet" nearly came all the way back to the pack in the Preakness however luckily for one Warren Merhrtens, the wire showed up a split-second ahead of Lord Boswell. Plying a much more patient ride in the Belmont, Merhrtens intently stalked behind a pacesetter named Natchez for nearly eleven furlongs before he launched the rally which impacted Paradise Farms' equine population.

While entirely legitimate, Assault's Triple Crown Championship was speedily belittled by cynics who resentfully pointed at three comparatively slow final times. (These haters also blasphemously dubbed thoroughbred racing's new magnate, "The best horse in a weak three-year old crop.") In the end though, Max Hirsch's effervescent student silenced his critics just two weeks after his coronation with a command performance in Belmont Park's Dwyer Stakes. Following a flop in the Arlington Classic (due to a kidney infection), the "Club Footed Comet" received a well deserved vacation however a subsequent string of five consecutive defeats compelled Robert J. Kleberg to "can" Warren Mehrtens.

In his first pairing with Assault, Eddie Arcaro procured the prestigious Pimlico Special by six lengths. Next it was onto Jamaica Racetrack where "The Master" and his new mount bewitchingly won the 1 3/16 mile Westchester Handicap. Tattooed with: a Triple Crown Championship, one particularly well timed late season comeback, unmatched purse earnings and a footnote detailing how in defeat he'd routinely given up weight to older racers, Assault's 1946 *résumé resultantly won over the panel responsible for electing America's "Three-Year Old Horse of the Year".*

A slave to his appetite, Assault therefore didn't bat an eye when Robert J. Kleberg barged in and bellowed, "Hey Max, I was just talking with Fitzsimmons and he told me that there's still one cargo car available on the 4:00 PM train to Jerome Park. Now do you want to start packing while I call the depot or vice versa?"

Simultaneous to Warren Mehrtens unexpected arrival, Hirsch cordially contended, "Um, I hate to break it to you Bob, but your horse is a bit below his training weight. What I'm saying is; I think we should stay put until I can pad his ribs a little. If he keeps packing it away like this though, the grind should start in about oh, nine or ten days."

"Nine or ten days!" Kleberg exasperatedly whined. "Well I had looked forward to breezing a bit sooner than that sir! Hmm, then again, you always know best. Now uh, I didn't get a chance to ask you after the Summit but, well, how do you think we fit in? You know, assuming he comes back at full strength."

Though reluctant to speculate past the next ten minutes, Assualt's pragmatic trainer nevertheless soothsaid, "With speedsters like: War Admiral, Sir Barton and Count Fleet in the mix there should be plenty of pace to close into. I mean if we get a clean trip, then I give us a puncher's chance."

As he tightly folded his arms, the "Club Footed Comet's" legal guardian groaned, "Ugh, I just keep thinking about the miracle we're going to need in order to outride Arcaro. O.K. well, since we're staying put for the time being, I'm gonna go ahead and kidnap *Homely* for a few hours. I don't have an appointment, but like their commercials say, 'Walk-ins are always welcome at "Damaris' Doggie Day Spa".'"

(Exceedingly loyal yet outwardly appalling, Homely the mutt had long been Assault's bosom buddy. Conceived somewhere on King Ranch, Paradise Farms' only "permitted pooch" was also a sort of good luck charm and therefore regularly received royal treatment.)

In the wake of Kleberg's departure, Warren Mehrtens fumed for a few seconds before he irately reverberated, *"I just keep thinking about the miracle we're going to need in order to outride Arcaro.* Boy there Bob; thanks for the vote of confidence!"

Knowing all too well that it wasn't always "wine and roses" between Assault's jockey and owner, Hirsch thus counseled, "Look son, you've heard the saying, '...like water off a duck's back'? Well you had better learn to live by it because I have absolutely no intention of playing referee for the next thirteen weeks!"

Presently flanked by their respective Champions in front of "Cargo Car #18", Earl Sande and Willie "Smokey"

Saunders now began to wonder if James Fitzsimmons would ever resurface. Ultimately vacating the restroom right as the 3:55 PM "all aboard" whistle blew, the soul Horse Racing Nation knew best as *"Sunny" Jim* next found himself literally face up with Omaha's belly button. Having been jerked high into the air because the *"Belair Bullet"* had suddenly reared, Saunders subsequently left his feet again when he heard Fitzsimmons holler, "Why didn't you sedate this basket-case like I ordered Willie?! Just look at him! Why he's wetter than Lake Erie!"

While he continued to wrestle with seventeen hands of raw irascibility, Omaha's jockey grievously alleged, "I did sir! He was fine until that infernal brass pipe boomed!"

"You're about to get a boom, a good one, from my steel-toe boot!" Fitzsimmons blared. "Now I want that stallion settled! And furthermore boy, lay off the cigars while onboard! Mr. Woodward won't get his deposit back if this jitney goes up in flames ya know!"

Totally used to his boss' discordant demeanor, Earl Sande therefore kept right on stroking Gallant Fox's supple snout while he gathered in, "Alright both of you listen up! I'll be out at Mr. Woodward's estate all day tomorrow discussing odds and ends but let's plan on inspecting Jerome Park's oval together first thing Wednesday morning, any questions?!"

Too scared to utter a word, Willie Saunders on that account simply nodded as he led Belair Stud's four-prong posse up Cargo Car #18's broad steel loading ramp. Opting to stick his arm out of an open slider window as the day's last convoy to Jerome Park pulled away from the station, Saunders' eventual good-bye wave to "Sunny" Jim was swiftly rebuked with, "Never mind me boy! Just keep an eye on that horse!"

Only because of a second tranquilizer (and a reverberating residency) was Omaha finally able to take advantage of his brand new super-scale memory foam travel mattress. Anything but sleepy (thanks to his late checkout from stall #2), Gallant Fox hence decided to take in the sights via Cargo Car #18's portside pane window. Standing high on his tip-toes with both ears pricked, thoroughbred racing's second Triple Crown Champion was soon rubbernecking like a college student who had left home for the very first time.

Now though normally jam packed with industrial payloads, Cargo Car #18 was presently masquerading as a portable equine Shangri-la. In fact, there was more than enough five-star grub and Finnish spring water on hand to sustain an entire herd yet for Belair's spoiled crew such excess was certainly nothing new. Truth be told, William Woodward Sr. often came under fire during the Great Depression because cynical newsmen would repeatedly print things like, *"Gallant Fox and Omaha are eating better than those millions of Americans who regularly say "grace" inside of government subsidized soup kitchens!"*

Once he was convinced that his mount was down for the count, Willie Saunders fired up a Diamond Crown Figurado #6 Cigar and then threw out, "Who would have ever thought it huh Earl? Father verses son for the whole caboodle!"

Through a three inch smirk, Sande sounded off, "Bro, we're the least of each other's problems! I mean have you forgotten that we're gonna be trading jabs with the likes of Secretariat and Citation?! I know one thing, we're gonna need all of the old man's magic this time around!"

"Can I please go five minutes without hearing someone mention those names?!" Saunders fussed. "Goodness gracious, the way everyone is talking, you'd think Jerome Park was hosting a match race! Man you know as well as I do Earl that any horse can win on any given day; ala *Jim Dandy*."

Seeing that he was eternally embittered towards any mention of the 100-1 shot who had famously upended Gallant Fox in the 1930 Travers Stakes, Sande thus threatened, "Keep it up pal and you'll be walking to Jerome Park!"

In back of apologetically waving his hands, Saunders chuckled, "Yeah that probably wasn't the best example. Well then, take Saratoga's other famous head scratcher, the 1973 Whitney Stakes!"

With a disbelieving voice, Sande reminisced, "The day *Onion* somehow knocked-off Secretariat. My goodness, only a forthcoming win by Omaha could top that upset!"

"Well hardy-ha-ha!" Saunders sarcastically crowed. "Just remember brother, you didn't think that we belonged going four thousand meters over the turf in the Ascot Gold Cup either! Such a shame *Quashed* ultimately clipped us, Woodward didn't deserve that."

Remembering said incident all too well, the "Fox of Belair's" bellwether therefore added, "No one deserves to

51

lose Europe's most storied race by a whisker Willie. And for the record, I didn't say that Omaha didn't belong. I only said that "jumping the pond" would probably take some starch out of him since he doesn't travel well."

As he stared down at the ponderous equine that was hibernating beneath his feet, Cargo Car #18's human chimney rambled, "You know Earl, I wasn't about to make a scene and embarrass Mr. Woodward in front of 150,000 people, however I honestly believe that bout at Royal Ascot was a draw. Oh man! Imagine if by some miracle this fray ended in a stalemate! Ha, why I can see the headline now, **"GALLANT FOX AND OMAHA DEAD HEAT FOR TOP HONORS IN HEAVEN'S PREMIER HORSE RACE!!!"**

While he kidnapped an ice cold bottle of Finnish spring water from Cargo Car #18's glass door refrigerator, Sande roared, "Dude, you're talking about something that would literally put Mr. Woodward over the moon for all of eternity!"

"What about you?" Saunders curiously solicited. "Would the sublime Earl Sande be content with sharing the "Sport of Kings'" utmost title?"

Subsequent to taking a swig of cool refreshment, Sande transparently divulged, "I wish I could say yes Willie, I wish I could say yes."

As he cordially waved Johnny Longden through the "four-way stop" that was located at the entrance of Paradise Farms' front parking lot, *George Conway* simultaneously turned up the volume on his vehicle's built-in GPS System. Soon harkening unto, *"Your estimated travel time is three hours and forty-six minutes,"* War Admiral's well-respected conditioner thereafter set Samuel D. Riddle's black and yellow "equine friendly" Winnebago on a collision course with Jerome Park. (Incidentally, Seattle Slew was also just seconds away from "flying the coup" by means of Mickey and Karen Taylor's customized 400 horsepower cream colored Cessna.)

Exiting his car slow so as not to ding Ariel's black Bentley, Johnny Longden next headed towards a pre-arranged 6:00 PM scheduling powwow with: Don Cameron, *Mr. John D. Hertz* and Count Fleet's owner, one *Mrs. John D.* (born *Fannie Kesner) Hertz*. Ever mindful that his mount's lovely master often exercised her feminine prerogative, Longden thus didn't turn a hair when he discovered a hand-written note on stall #6's front door which read,

ARRIVED EARLY BUT THEN RECEIVED A CALL FROM FANNIE SAYING THAT SHE WANTED ME TO MEET HER AND JOHN OVER AT JEROME PARK. I'M GUESSING SHE WANTS TO ASSESS THE BARNS AND OVAL BEFORE WE SHIP. I CALLED YOU BUT YOUR PHONE WENT TO VOICEMAIL. I'LL BE IN TOUCH TOMORROW MORNING WITH WHATEVER PLAN WE DRAW UP.

-DON

After kicking himself for not "un-silencing" his smart-phone, Johnny Longden turned his attention towards those reddened hues that were rinsing over every inch of Paradise Farms' Core Meadow. Figuring a scenic stroll would help wash his blues away, Count Fleet's disenchanted jockey hence ambled along until he ran smack dab into some familiar faces. Grinning as he accepted Penny Chenery's cheery hello, Longden then eyeballed Secretariat and said, "I must say ma'am, he looks even better than advertised. Uh, think you can give the rest of us a head start?!"

With a troubled inflection, Chenery tiresomely published, "Unfortunately that's a given Johnny, in terms of getting to Jerome Park at least. Truth is our fella is running a slight fever so we're effectively grounded for the time being. You know and honestly, I don't like how much he's been outside today but like my trainer always says, 'There's no use fighting him Penny, "Big Red" goes wherever and does whatever he wants!'"

"Well he certainly proved that in the Preakness!" Longden cackled. "And honest to goodness ma'am, the replay of your runner prematurely rushing to the lead on Pimlico's first turn always gives me chills. Gee willikers, why *Ron* must have thought that his mount had gone mad!"

Subsequent to putting her smile back on, Secretariat's stately owner extolled, "Ninety-nine out of one hundred jockeys would have gathered in the reins! *Mr. Turcotte* however was wise enough to just sit back and go with the flow. Mm, if he hadn't, Heaven's Premier Horse Race might only have ten entrants!"

In that he was as clear cut as they came, Longden told, "Well there's no arguing about one thing, most who share my profession do love to micro-manage! I mean I used

54

to always see speedsters get pulled back or worse, boys who would try to make the lead on a dead closer. You know what I used to tell young jockeys who came to me looking for advice ma'am? I'd say, 'Number one, hang on! And number two, stay out of your horse's way!'"

"Yes, oftentimes less is more." Chenery chirped. "And uh, speaking of sound decision making, I should probably take my convalescent home now sir. The angels around here start stressing out if the boarders aren't tucked in by nightfall you know."

Interlude - Trapped in a Moment

After staying behind for a few minutes so he could watch the stars come out, Johnny Longden retreated back towards the irreplaceable treasure that was stabled inside of stall #6. (Now mind you, Count Fleet was nearly unloaded to another horseman for a measly $4500 early on in 1942. However in the end, Johnny Longden's persuasive plea of, "Don't sell him sir, he just hasn't matured yet!" prevented John D. Hertz from making the biggest mistake of his life.)

Spanning less than one full year, Count Fleet's career ironically culminated on the very stage where he "earned his wings". See, at the beginning of the Belmont Stakes, Fannie Hertz's hot-rod suffered a left-front ankle injury that just never quite resolved itself. Perpetually "stuck in the past" concerning this incident, Johnny Longden consequently revisited all the things that could have been as he closed in on the Primary Barn.

Fresh off his dinner break, a soul simply known as *"Mr. Sam"* was now in the process of sweeping away some silt that had accumulated near stall #6's front entrance. Soon attending his buddy's bemoaning, Count Fleet's steadfast groom tolerantly took in an ear-full before he asserted, "O.K. yes, his career down there came to an end all to soon but believe me Johnny, in three months time he'll own the only title that matters. I can feel it in my bones I tell ya! Yep, our guy is gonna show them all! Even that "Don Juan" you were just kissing up to out there!"

Feeling like he'd been categorized with *Judas*, Longden resultantly made a face and then contended, "I wasn't kissing up. I was being polite. And uh, before you question my loyalty pal, let me ask you something; who always talks about how our guy's twenty-five length Belmont Stakes rout on a bum ankle compares with Secretariat's thirty-one length score?"

While he continued to push his corn broom back and forth, Mr. Sam came back with, "And who always reminds you that the rest of Horse Racing Nation will never see it that way since the Count only faced two rivals in New York."

"Honestly, I was surprised that anyone drew in at all!" Longden laughed. "Shoot, why even our unassuming boss fell into shock when she found out that there were

actually two owners in the wings with nerve enough face
us!"

Chapter 3 - Jerome Park

Two blocks away from the theater that would stage Heaven's Premier Horse Race, a waitress whose magenta blouse read, *"Bathsheba's Bistro"* now started to clear away Commander J.K.L. Ross' and H.G. Bedwell's barren breakfast dishes. Soon shifting focus to a page in his day-timer that was tabbed *"Sep. 27th"*, Sir Barton's stuffed trainer then scribbled away until he heard an inpatient voice say, "C'mon Harvey, let's go check out our new headquarters. You can finish up that to-do list later on this afternoon."

In back of pulling into an empty space inside of Heaven's only seven story sterling silver parking garage, H.G. Bedwell and Commander J.K.L. Ross excitedly stepped onto the 10kt gold brick footpath that filtered into Jerome Park's sprawling backside. Colorfully illuminated courtesy of daybreak, this seven acre clearing was definitely in a class by itself in that it contained a horizontal row of eleven 2000 sq. ft. "Equine Chateaus". Partitioned (and shaded) by giant palm trees, every "guest bungalow" stationed behind the "King of Wall Street's" virgin oval was likewise symmetrically skirted with (no kidding) a half-acre partially fenced-in flood irrigated foraging field!

Already settled inside of Equine Chateau #1, Sir Barton was thus fringed by 1,234 slats of black walnut paneling. Now though conferred every single creature comfort a horse could ever want, Commander J.K.L. Ross' Champion had fallen especially in love with his new pad's double layer of "hoof friendly" memory foam flooring. (Topped off with two thousand gallons of mineral infused spring water, Equine Chateau #1's turbo-jet rectangular hot tub was another amenity that Sir Barton's haggard hooves would grow to love.)

Because he knew that being a racehorse's primary care giver meant being on-call 24/7, Leonard Jerome had kindly embellished each Equine Chateau with an adjoining "Groom's Chamber". Accessible via a keyless side entrance, these attached studio cottages also boasted: a twin bed, one bitty dining table, a mini-fridge, cable television a fifteen hundred station satellite stereo and a bathroom that came with: name-brand travel-size toiletries, a space saving glass shower and an antique pedestal style marble vanity.

Though they had come through Equine Chateau #1's horizontally divided front door praising Jerome Park's "back of house" area, Commander J.K.L. Ross' and H.G. Bedwell courteously "kept a lid on it" as Toots Thompson wrapped up a comprehensive ten point pre-conditioning examination. Twice as knowledgeable as most licensed trainers, Thompson was therefore an invaluable intangible yet if it hadn't been for "the man in the brown suit and black derby", Sir Barton's death would have almost certainly preceded his professional ascension. (That said, when Commander J.K.L. Ross tried to thank him for weeding out his bad-tempered animal's blood poisoning, H.G. Bedwell lifted a hand and then emphatically insisted, "It was only that mule's sheer stubbornness which staved off the Grim Reaper sir.")

Once he had packed up his "fine tooth comb", Thompson perplexedly conveyed, "Well gents, even though I can't pinpoint anything particular he seems a little lethargic; jetlag maybe?"

"It's entirely possible." Bedwell answered. "No biggie though, he'll likely perk up once the blood starts flowing. Now what about Mr. Bishop Toots? I'm assuming he's already been by?"

As he dug a piece of spearmint chewing gum out of his pocket, Sir Barton's versatile groom updated, "He walked in at 5:30, did his thing, and was gone before I could say 'thank you'. Nice enough fella though. Shoes look great too. Oh and by the way boss, I filled those steel buckets over near the hot tub up with mud for later on."

After he had tested the consistency of said muck with his index finger, Equine Chateau #1's creative conditioner noted, "He always looks so silly standing in this stuff but hey, more moisture equals less hoof cracks. Uh, by the way Toots, where is Loftus hiding?"

In the midst of blowing a tiny bubble, Thompson distortedly responded, "Out near the gap sir." *(A "slidable" section of outer rail that was located at the very head of the backstretch, "the gap" was essentially, "the official gateway to Jerome Park's racing surface".)*

Turned-off by the idea of marching to the end of shed row and back, Bedwell hence huffed, "I'll just brief him when we get out there then. Go ahead now and grab me an exercise saddle Toots."

Though he'd cut out with the intention of sneaking a quick peek at the "playing field", Johnny Loftus was now thirty minutes into drooling over eternity's most spectacular sporting amphitheater. Stretching the entire length of the straightaway, Jerome Park's one hundred meter tall, double-tiered Main Grandstand had been painstakingly fitted together with 375,000 metric tons of polished white Italian calacatta marble. Buttressed from left to right with thirty-five massive cylindrical support pillars, Leonard Jerome's recreational monstrosity likewise possessed a facial 14kt gold "maximum occupancy" plaque which read, **"CAPACITY 200,000"**.

Connecting "Level 1" and "Level 2", the Main Grandstand's center circular staircase fantastically showcased a total of five hundred decorative 14kt gold banister posts. Weighing approximately 100 lbs. apiece, each of these coiled pillars was beautifully capped with an eight inch 14kt gold handcrafted thoroughbred horse head. (A veracious admirer of the thoroughbred athlete, Leonard Jerome had therefore also footed the bill to fill every surrounding stadium alcove with either a turf related: tapestry, sculpture or oil painting.)

Installed via aluminum flag poles twenty-four hours prior, eleven "tribute banners" could now be seen atop the Main Grandstand's vaulted Spanish clay tile rooftop. Arranged in chronological order from left to right, Heaven's swankiest collection of customized silk pennants individually brandished: a particular Triple Crown Champion's name, their likeness and their "year of conquest".

In front of the Main Grandstand (at the edge of an extensive apron that was paved with solid silver bricks) was where one could find Jerome Park's Winner's Enclosure. (Situated just past the finish line, the seventy meter circumference, pearl gated, longed for final destination of those locking horns on New Year's Eve had actually been upgraded in recent weeks to include 22kt gold cobblestone and a four foot high diamond encrusted perimeter wall!)

Carpeted with what Loftus presumed was Zoysia grass, Jerome Park's perfectly manicured infield paraded a virtual sea of undulating rises. (FYI - although Heaven's Premier Horse Race would naturally unfold over the "King of Wall Street's" eight furlong sandy loam cushioned all-weather dirt course, there was also an interior seven furlong Kentucky fescue turf track on site!) Now set about five meters behind this grass oval's front side inner rail was the largest tote board that Johnny Loftus had ever laid eyes on. One hundred meters long and taller than a giraffe on stilts, the foreground's mountainous odds panel was moreover bookended by two elevated 60x40 meter 4k race-play video screens!

Totally consumed with looking to and fro, Sir Barton's preoccupied pilot thus jumped back a pace when, from out of nowhere, he heard his trainer say, "Quite a sight eh Johnny?"

"It is indeed sir!" Loftus yelped. "Goodness sakes, just look at that Clubhouse!"

In back of heeding his rider's outstretched finger, H.G. Bedwell fervidly fish-eyed the four column fifty-one room Victorian Mansion that was situated just behind Jerome Park's first turn. (Set on a rise that could be climbed via eleven 14kt gold steps, the "King of Wall Street's" manor in fact matched the color of those on scene Cumulous clouds since it was made entirely from synthetic ivory.)

A towering three-tier 14kt gold fountain, one that was surrounded by eleven full-scale rearing 14kt gold thoroughbred busts, fantastically crowned the Clubhouse's Main Courtyard. Uniformly turned inward, those pseudo racers who loitered on Leonard Jerome's front lawn had also been fitted with spouts which allowed them to continuously expel eleven upward streams of sparkling spring water!

In an effort to put the task at hand ahead of casual sightseeing, Bedwell hurriedly stepped backwards while he decreed, "C'mon son make haste; Toots is waiting to give you a leg up."

Following a quick pivot, Johnny Loftus determinedly approached his helpmate however in that instant where Thompson heaved, the gap's vinegary racer took off like a shot. Subsequent to thanking his *Creator* that Bedwell had been able to snag Sir Barton's bridle as it bustled by, Loftus rose to one knee and then hypothesized, "He's been a civilian for way too long boss. Looks like we're gonna have to break him all over again."

"Break him?!" Bedwell cried. "Hey, I don't have time to re-teach him his ABCs Johnny! Now you're gonna jog this animal two miles today if I have to lash you to his back!"

Though he was in no hurry to get KO'd again, Loftus obediently embraced his sworn duty until Thompson called out, "Hang tight gentlemen, we don't have the right of way."

Responsible for successfully channeling War Admiral through the 1937 Triple Crown Series, jockey *Charlie Kurtsinger* now rocketed his mount past the gap while he simultaneously ribbed, "Should I go grab an icepack for your bottom there Johnny?!"

Back on the apron, Samuel D. Riddle made two tight fists and then screamed, "George Conway, what is the meaning of this charade?! I said I wanted him eased, eased into training!"

With the meekest voice he could muster, Conway justified, "He was all kinds of rank as I walked him down the backside too sir. I think these new surroundings have got him a little excited."

"I'd call this a bit more than rank man!" Riddle bawled. "Now tell Charlie to slow down! That's an order!"

As he stepped towards the fifty-six inch tall 14kt gold post fence that separated Jerome Park's apron and outer rail, George Conway simultaneously executed a "throat-slash" sign. Now despite those scathing physical repercussions that would result from hastily dropping anchor, Charlie Kurtsinger nevertheless "downshifted" as he rounded Jerome Park's far turn. (You see, trying to pull up War Admiral was like trying to stop a Mack Truck that was traveling downhill on an icy interstate and therefore, Kurtsinger's biceps were no stranger to decent sized stress tears.)

No longer satisfied with being a bystander, Commander J.K.L. Ross thus aided his team's cause by bracing Sir Barton's squirming backside. Successful in boarding his "Brahma Bull" the second time around, Loftus then tightly clutched the reins as H.G. Bedwell went on with,

"O.K. Johnny, like I said, just two light counterclockwise laps so we can start knocking some of the rust off of him. Oh, and steer clear of the Admiral! The last thing I need is Riddle reading me the riot act!"

In that they wanted to secure a head on view of Sir Barton's second go around, H.G. Bedwell and Commander J.K.L. Ross soon set their sights on Jerome Park's twenty-five hundred square meter paddock. (Located behind the outer rail right where the backstretch and far turn intersected, the 14kt gold gated "prep area" for Heaven's Premier Horse Race was actually beautifully scented thanks to eleven sequentially numbered Ceylon Cedar saddling stalls. Additionally, because it stood some seventy-five meters tall and was planted square in the center of the paddock's half-furlong three meter wide 14kt gold brick walking ring, Jerome Park's quadruple sided turquoise clock tower could be plainly read from anywhere on property!)

While he watched Sir Barton zigzag past like he was "three sheets to the wind", H.G. Bedwell detailed, "He's drifting in and out like that due to fatigue sir but don't worry, in two weeks time I'll have him going as straight as a string."

In back of dialing up the most unconcerned tone imaginable, Ross maintained, "You didn't win America's training title six years in a row by accident Harvey."

Interlude - Commander J.K.L Ross

On that occasion where he was cornered by a newspaper columnist who asked, "Can you characterize your boss' personality in a dozen words or less?" H.G. Bedwell had unsmilingly answered, "He is a serious minded soul who never hands out hollow praise."

Certainly all business all the time, Commander J.K.L. Ross' inherited fortune had actually helped establish the "Canadian Pacific Railroad" (however it was an intrinsic zeal for both thoroughbred horse racing and nautical exploration which motivated Sir Barton's staid owner to get out of bed in the morning). Now though obviously more renowned for his turf pedigree, Ross "the yachtsman" had in fact been recruited by the Royal Yacht Squadron at Cowes, England! (This is an honor on par with that of induction into the American Jockey Club.)

A dyed-in-the-wool gambler, Commander J.K.L. Ross would truly wager on anything under the sun yet no bet ever compared to the great "Derby Dare" of 1919. (Totally convinced that Eternal would get the better of Billy Kelly in the "Run for the Roses", noted gambler Arnold Rothstein (yes, the same soul who fixed Major League Baseball's 1919 World Series) had therefore approached Ross with terms pertaining to a $50,000 "heads-up" proposition! Note: since Billy Kelly (as previously mentioned) wound up finishing in second place behind Sir Barton, Rothstein was unable to take advantage of an agreed upon clause which stipulated, "Said wager will terminate if both racers finish worse than third.")

As he walked his winded mount up alongside the paddock, Johnny Loftus weighed in, "You saw the late wear but otherwise, he went o.k. boss."

Because he had nothing to add, H.G. Bedwell consequently commanded, "Go cool him down and when you see Toots, pass along that we'll start with about ninety minutes of mud."

Once he was back alone with Sir Barton's conditioner, Commander J.K.L. Ross brought his eyes around towards Jerome Park's turquoise clock tower and then said, "If you had to guess Harvey, what do you think his odds will be?"

Now even though pari-mutual pools were the furthest thing from his mind, Bedwell nevertheless estimated, "Assuming he comes back at full strength, I see him at around 15-1 on the morning line. But what does it matter sir? You know you can't bet on him."

In the course of opening the wee platinum canister of Count Murari snuff that was always on his person, Commander J.K.L. Ross muttered, "Hmm yes, forgive me sir, I guess old habits die hard."

Chapter 4 - Now Open to the Public

The consequence of being caressed by a faint southeast breeze, Citation suddenly woke from the restful post-breakfast nap he'd been taking alongside Paradise Farms' far off hot spring. Invariably spot on, "Big Cy's" horse sense currently told that a physical transplant was imminent however for the time being, it was all about the passionate pursuit of relaxation. (Actually inclined to start a little hydrotherapy, thoroughbred racing's eighth Triple Crown Champion now rolled over so that he could formally acquaint his body with some ninety-nine and a half degree "Adam's ale".)

Two miles away beside the Primary Barn's fifth stall, the soul who was responsible for outfitting Warren Wright Sr. with four Kentucky Derby Championships had set his focus on page 1 of a brand new hardback conditioning journal. Now though his principal claim to fame could be summed up in the title of "Head Trainer for Lexington, Kentucky's Calumet Farms from 1940-1947", Ben Jones had also successfully mentored his son (a son who by the way, voluntarily fought in World War II during what would've been the prime of his career). Promoted to "Head Trainer" when his father inherited the role of "Calumet Farms' General Manager" in 1948, Jimmy Jones ultimately became the first thoroughbred conditioner in history to accumulate over $1,000,000 in purse monies.

One who would spend the next three months telling himself, *"Anything can happen once those gates open,"* Ben Jones nevertheless believed in his heart of hearts that Heaven's Premier Horse Race was absolutely Citation's to lose. (Arguably the "Sport of Kings'" best ever three-year old, "Big Cy's" only loss from twenty starts in 1948 occurred on April 12th in the Chesapeake Trial Stakes at Harve de Grace Racetrack. Quick to disregard this race because a high-strung horse named *Hefty* had interfered with half the field, James Fitzsimmons thereafter insistently went on record with, "Up to this point Citation's done more than any horse I ever saw, and I saw Man o' War.")

As he looked up into the rangy shadow that had abruptly come over him, Ben Jones digested, "Mr. Wright gave the go ahead so I booked our boys on tomorrow's 7:00 AM train like we talked about Pop."

Wishing to grant the courtesy of eye contact, "Mr. Longtail's" trainer on that account took off his teardrop aviator sunglasses before he shot back, "7:00 AM it is then. Uh, now what did the boss say about our other dialogue?"

With no beating around the bush, Jimmy Jones reported, "He wholeheartedly agreed that you and I should just stick to what we know best rather than try to co-manage things. I mean like you said Pop, we can seek each other out for advice if need be however once we transplant, I'll call the shots concerning Citation. Likewise, you'll have the last word when it comes to Whirlaway. Oh hey and I wanted to let you know that Jerome Park's resident veterinarian got back to me about that voicemail I left. Real nice fellow; said he'd be more than happy to run by with his portable x-ray machine tomorrow afternoon."

Because he was now being blinded by the intense mid-morning glare that was coming up from Paradise Farms' Core Meadow, Ben Jones put his shades back on before he recapped, "Well like I said, "Big Cy's" arthritis has likely dissipated by now, however I certainly can't blame you for putting him through a comprehensive ankle scan."

Interlude - Calumet Farms' One-Two Punch

Even though he'd been much more "hands on" with Citation ahead of the 74th "Run for the Roses", Jimmy Jones had insisted that his father be written in as "Big Cy's" official conditioner. You see at the time, only Herbert J. "Derby Dick" Thompson had readied four Kentucky Derby Champions however Citation ultimately helped knot a "trainer's tie" which lasted until Ponder (a 16-1 pari-mutual improbable) handed Ben Jones an unprecedented fifth Kentucky Derby title in 1949. For the record, Ben Jones took Louisville by storm for the sixth and final time in 1952 with the heavily favored Hill Gail.

Technically credited with training two Kentucky Derby Champions, Jimmy Jones' duo of captors are pictured in Webster's Dictionary beside the word "dissimilar". Now on one hand there's Iron Liege, an 8-1 shot who was basically handed the blanket of roses in 1957 because jockey Bill Shoemaker (who was aboard Gallant Man) misjudged where Churchill Downs' finish line was. Secondly, we have Tim Tam, a brilliant thoroughbred who lost the 1958 Belmont Stakes (and with it a Triple Crown Championship) on account of a freakish leg injury which occurred one furlong from the wire.

Speaking not out of politeness but because he was sincerely interested in both halves of Calumet's operation, Jimmy Jones first shooed away a hovering dragonfly ahead of probing, "Hey uh, now that you've been able to spend a little quality time with him, how does Whirlaway look Pop?"

While he twisted his neck back towards stall #5, Ben Jones confirmed, "A bit soft from being on the shelf, but that's an easy fix because he's a glutton for work. Confidentially son, it's his age-old penchant to waft off course which well, worries me some."

Since he truly believed that no retiree ever completely shed their on-track education, Citation's supervisor encouraged, "Well, he might make off here and there however I don't think you'll have to start back at square one Pop."

"Let's hope not 'cause I don't know if these old bones are up to that." Calumet's senior conditioner sighed. "At any rate, have you touched base with Butch and Sundance about tomorrow?"

Old friends with a cabdriver who worked the bar scene, Jimmy Jones was therefore aware that the rather "plastered" pair of Eddie Arcaro and Al Snider had been dropped off in front of Bathsheba's Bistro at 8:00 AM. Pretty sure his father would have a coronary if he found out that Calumet's jockeys were currently "feeling no pain", Jimmy Jones thus casually lied, "I'll give them both a call a little later on this afternoon Pop."

Behind taking on the tone of a Marine Core drill sergeant, Ben Jones specified, "Tell those rascals to be at the station with their gloves on by 6:30 AM! No doubt it'll take all four of us to get Whirlaway up that loading ramp!"

As he parted ways with Paradise Farms via his 1966 sea green Studebaker, Jimmy Jones looked back on an often told (yet far from old) turf anecdote. The scene was the 1941 Kentucky Derby and although he simply appeared to be at peace with himself inside of Churchill Downs' paddock, Eddie Arcaro actually couldn't do without the wooden wall he was leaning up against. Now in truth, Al Snider probably wouldn't attempt to emulate his good friend by riding with a hangover however with all that was on the line, it was certainly better to be safe than sorry.

Though he purposefully stalled out halfway across Bathsheba's Bistro in order to admire the way Al Snider was using the Eternity Times' morning edition as a pillow, Jimmy Jones eventually sidled up alongside table #12 with an acknowledgement of, "Morning there Eddie."

Since he never let anything come between him and a second breakfast course, "The Master" kept right on buttering his cornbread while he reciprocated, "Morning Jimmy! Oh, never mind Snider here. We were out late last night celebrating his comeback. C'mon and sit down; I'll buy you a cup of coffee."

Once he had taken a load off, table #12's concerned caller began to explain, "Look Eddie, I came here because..."

"Like I don't know why you're here." Arcaro laughingly interrupted, "You're afraid I'm leading him down the road of destruction. Well you're getting yourself all in a tizzy for nothing man. Know what he kept saying to me until he passed out? He kept saying, 'No more sauce after tonight Eddie. Starting tomorrow, I'm gonna be tucked in by 8:00 PM!' I believe him too Jimmy. Trust me brother, Snider wants to win this thing more than you ever will. Guaranteed, he'll absolutely walk the line once the heavy lifting starts."

After he'd taken "The Master" at his word, Calumet's junior conditioner communicated, "Well for your information it starts tomorrow, literally. See, our boys are booked on the 7:00 AM train to Jerome Park and since loading Whirlaway isn't exactly a one man job, Pop wants everyone at the station with their gloves on by half past six."

As he carefully slipped the Eternity Times' morning edition out from underneath his good pal's lax noggin, "The Master" promised, "I'll pass that info along to sleeping beauty here. Now check this out man, there is a panoramic picture of Jerome Park and an article about Heaven's Premier Horse Race right on the front page!"

Comfortably seated at the oblong stained glass table that dominated his Clubhouse's second story veranda,

Leonard Jerome now considered both the apron's dense population, and a certain "buried" $1000 bill. Although suddenly sidetracked from the goings-on below (because his upstairs butler had shown up with five brunch crepes and a fresh pot of Columbian coffee), the "King of Wall Street" nonetheless became business orientated again inside of that moment where August Belmont walked up and announced, "Look old boy, look! Turner is giving *Mr. Cruget* a leg up behind the gap!"

Whereas he was equally interested in stuffing his stomach, Jerome spun the lid off a jar of fresh strawberry preserves before he asked, "The Taylors are in close proximity I assume?"

"They've got their smart phones out and are ready to film!" Belmont familiarized.

Quickly caving into his curiosity, Jerome resultantly reached for the binoculars that "lived" on his veranda's most exquisite piece of furniture. Soon with an up-close view of the action, the "King of Wall Street" was thus able to meticulously watch Mickey Taylor record Billy Turner for posterity as he briefed, "Don't gallop him faster than ten miles per hour today *Jean*. When dealing with this kind of layoff, you've got to bring them back incrementally."

Interlude - Discovering a Diamond in the Rough

Born with spindly chicken legs, Seattle Slew also fell out of his mama with a voluminous head that was exceedingly disproportionate to an otherwise medial frame. Consequently, it came as a startling surprise when veterinarian Jim Hill (an astute appraiser of horseflesh and a close friend of both Mickey and Karen Taylor) recommended "rolling the dice". (Ultimately acquired at auction for a paltry $17,500, the "Sport of Kings'" tenth Triple Crown Champion is on that account "thoroughbred horse racing's version of a winning lottery ticket"!)

After Seattle Slew broke his maiden at first asking at Saratoga Race Course, a leading local conditioner appeared on the backside with a "worthwhile" certified check in his hand. Already suspecting that they'd caught lightning in a bottle, Mickey and Karen Taylor therefore gustily turned down a trade that would have made them exactly $300,000 richer! Now although the Taylor's turbo-charged equine subsequently annihilated an allowance field, a record breaking 9 3/4 length romp in Belmont Park's 106ᵗʰ Champagne Stakes was Seattle Slew's real coming out party.

Feeling nostalgic because he was finally back in the saddle, Jean Cruget for that reason dug up a daring doing which had brought him both everlasting acclaim and stark criticism. Carried away emotionally because he was atop the very first horse that had ever made it through the Triple Crown Series without a single loss, Cruget hence stood up and saluted Belmont Park's saturated grandstand. (The problem with this you ask? Well, many fans (call them crazy) believe that a jockey shouldn't start celebrating until they actually cross the wire.)

Interlude - Hard as Nails

Toughened by an arduous adolescence, Jean Cruget's mental resolve had always proved to be an invaluable intangible for "Team Slew". (Undeniably, parental discourse and isolation within the confines of an orphanage would thicken anyone's skin.) Making the rest of his dark days seem like one giant birthday party, Cruget's most demanding role had definitely been that of a French soldier, one who saw prolonged action in the savage Algerian War.

The product of finally seeing some hastened horseflesh, Jerome Park's guest population now energetically crowded up against the apron's fifty-six inch tall 14kt gold post fence. Of course as one might expect, the air was soon thick with opinion concerning Seattle Slew's win probability however rather than augment the surrounding noise pollution, *Pomeroy J. Mandalay* kept his "two cents' worth" between himself and a Windsor tan workout diary. Suddenly recognized for who he really was (i.e., the most gifted thoroughbred handicapper who had ever walked the face of the Earth), Mandalay thus heeded a friendly tap on the shoulder and the words, "Well if it isn't the man who put down ten thousand to win on *Dark Star*! You know that was the single greatest bet I ever booked in my fifty-one years behind the cage! Gosh, what does that feel like fella? I mean, to turn ten dimes into a quarter million?!"

While he obviously remembered (and could accurately relate) every single detail of the 1953 "Kentucky Derby killing" that had catapulted him in a much higher tax bracket, Pomeroy J. Mandalay was likewise the sort who preferred privacy over praise. For this reason, *"Paradise's premier handicapper"* quickly hatched a forgery and then fibbed, "Ten thousand dollars?! You've got the wrong guy pal. Shoot, half the time my piggybank hasn't got ten cents in its belly!"

After taking the hint, the apron's nosey parker shrewdly attempted to extract some educated pari-mutuel dope by casually chitchatting, "My apologies sir. Seems I have you mixed up with someone else. I'll tell you what though; you don't have to be a turf guru in order to recognize the quality of Seattle Slew. Not to mention, he's the value play of this whole shindig! I mean, when you consider the amount of coin that's gonna ride on Secretariat and Citation, why, that in itself will grant me 4-1 on a horse who went 14 for 17 lifetime!"

Morphing into *Mr. Hyde* in those times when he sensed any sort of "odds discrepancy", the apron's prime punter hence flared, "Ha, 4-1 my eye! Man assuming no one scratches, then I'd bet my gold molar that you'll get 9/2 on your money!"

Overheard by more than one eavesdropper, Mandalay's pari-mutual prognostication remained "the talk of the town" up until that moment when an observant bystander bellowed, "Hey, check out the gap! Woodward's entire crew is coming out alongside two of Mr. Jerome's work horses!"

First taking up his nickel plated brass binoculars, Pomeroy J. Mandalay thereupon read William Woodward Sr.'s lips as they told, "Away we go 'eh gents? Mr. Fitzsimmons, it's your show sir."

Interlude - The Brains Behind Belair Stud

A quintessential blue-blood of infallible lineage, William Woodward Sr. attended Groton School in Massachusetts prior to graduating from Harvard Law School in 1901. Subsequent to serving in Great Britain as a U.S. ambassador, Woodward inherited the deed to both Hanover National Bank (NY) and Maryland's majestic "Belair Estate" (a splendid equine nirvana where horses had been turned out to stud for well over two centuries). The sort who placed very little value on two-year old racing, Woodward instead consistently pointed his stock towards a select assemblage of American and British Classics.

Now contrary to Seattle Slew (who wouldn't even break a sweat), Gallant Fox and Omaha were staring directly down the barrel of an abrupt "baptism by fire". As "old school" as they came, James Edward Fitzsimmons believed in working his horses hard and often yet no dose of concentrated conditioning had ever been able to completely cure the acute weirdness that went on between the "Fox of Belair's" fuzzy ears. See, thoroughbred racing's second Triple Crown Champion loved to: crowd his competition, decelerate when he made the lead and (worse of all) unconcernedly stargaze. (Truth be told, Earl Sande's mount once completely missed the break in a stakes race at Belmont Park all because he was spying a low flying plane!)

The fact that he was being implanted against the inner rail across from the gap didn't stop Gallant Fox from keeping an eye on the exercise rider who was now lining up his chocolate colored stallion alongside the "half mile pole". *(Half mile pole - A vertical indicator located on the inner backstretch which stands exactly four furlongs (one half mile) from the finish line.)* Staying true to his rubbernecking nature, the "Fox of Belair" next put both pupils on the blonde haired and blue eyed exercise rider that was targeting Jerome Park's "three-eighths marker". Releasing Omaha's bridle once both sparring partners had dug in, Fitzsimmons subsequently dictated, "O.K. Willie, take this bundle of nerves down to the top of the homestretch."

Turning into a bit of a worry wart himself as the "Belair Bullet" migrated south, William Woodward Sr.

resultantly stepped forward and then second guessed, "I must admit James, I'm fearful that they're not ready for such an aggressive move."

After he'd wiped away some bothersome brow sweat with a white handkerchief, "Sunny" Jim justified, "You always tell me to trust my intuition sir. It follows then that we jump in with both feet."

Utilized by horsemen for generations, the maneuver that was about to shake up Jerome Park simultaneously instilled both cardiovascular endurance and something a sports psychologist would call "competitive confidence". (Basically present to be "punching bags" for Belair's titans, the strip's exercise riders would accordingly break off at only half speed once Gallant Fox got within forty yards of them.) Interested primarily in the upcoming drill's third and final phase, Pomeroy J. Mandalay therefore went and titled a clean diary page with the heading, *Gallant Fox vs. Omaha - Round 1*".

Although there was a massive metal sign near the gap which particularized, "**Jerome Park's racing surface is a communal resource rightly belonging to all competing parties.**" James Fitzsimmons didn't want to mobilize his crew until a certain dark bay horse withdrew. Now despite being boring at best to those on the apron, Seattle Slew's incipient jaunt around Jerome Park had put one Billy Turner in high spirits. Having felt first-hand what his trainer had witnessed, Jean Cruget consequently came through the gap saying, "I forgot that this guy doesn't run boss, he floats."

At that point where there was no longer a chance of impeding Mickey and Karen Taylor's "airy Champion", James Fitzsimmons confidently gave Earl Sande his cue. (Not far down the road, Pomeroy J. Mandalay hastily penned, *"GF - Away clean, good early speed, but "wandering" everywhere."*) Ultimately deciding not to take pains over the dust a prolonged shelf life had imparted, Sande instead concentrated on how easily he was hooking the strip's chocolate colored stallion.

Since the ground beneath him had literally begun to shake, Willie Saunders figured it was the right time to turn the ignition key. Brought to life by both Omaha's flight and the sight of Gallant Fox blowing past yet another overmatched adversary, William Woodward Sr. on that account hollered, "Hold onto your overalls James!"

Even though Willie Saunders' edgy mount was up against it from a momentum standpoint, Pomeroy J. Mandalay knew that Gallant Fox's "hat trick" wouldn't come easy. (And as predicted, Omaha fought with hammer and tongs over what Mandalay would later chronicle as, *"two hotly contested furlongs".*) Finally able to tear his Champion's wandering eyes off of the Main Grandstand, Sande in turn wrested a last second burst which helped him get home first (albeit by the width of a wine glass stem).

Consistent with how they had crossed the wire, William Woodward's twosome remained inseparable as they galloped out around Jerome Park's clubhouse turn. Forced to vocally adapt because the apron's population had completely erupted, James Fitzsimmons thus encased his mouth with two cupped hands before he cried, "Let's get Omaha in first position now Willie! Earl, you get topside!"

Seeing as how he still had the jitters, Omaha steadily rocked back and forth as he watched his papa parade past the oval's repositioned workhorses. Now although the "Belair Bullet" ultimately came around the bend looking a little "green", Earl Sande wasn't fooled into thinking that it was game over. Sure enough, those crowding the apron soon witnessed almost an exact replay of Gallant Fox's initial microscopic score.

One who never wasted an opportunity to poke fun, Sande therefore stood up in the irons out past the wire and then needled, "Whoo hoo! Now that's how I like to start my day Willie, by going two for two!"

"Oh you're batting a thousand!" Saunders snidely shouted back. "Yes sir, by a combined distance of two and a half centimeters!"

Once he'd congratulated William Woodward Sr. on a satisfactory commencement, "Sunny" Jim told his incoming squad, "Take 'em back in boys! And you can tell our grooms, 'The old man wants them cooled out for forty minutes, and then scrubbed from head to toe!'"

As William Woodward Sr.'s duo began their voyage back towards the barn area, Leonard Jerome weakened the worth of his Giant Squid skin billfold by exactly $1000. In back of sizing up the apron's substantial citizenry one final time, the "King of Wall Street" faced August Belmont and then graciously put forth, "Well, here are your winnings old boy. Mm, you know, I just really didn't think that more than a few hundred people would show up this morning."

While he squirreled away his business partner's pocket change, Belmont gently rubbed in, "Remember what

I said before we bet Leonard? Uh, I quote, 'If you open up during training hours, Horse Racing Nation will flood in here by the thousands to see their heroes.' Plus, this is a workday! I mean, can you imagine the crowds we'll have come the weekend?! And now not to damper the mood but, I think this turnout has perhaps warned us that Jerome Park's seating capacity is not even close to what it needs to be."

Chapter 5 - The Prophetic Pays a Visit

Even though Fannie Hertz had incessantly praised Leonard Jerome's lustrous facility throughout her preliminary walk through, Count Fleet could still feel the breeze coming up from Paradise Farms' Core Meadow. See, Heaven's pickiest horsewoman had refused to let her Champion be the "guinea pig" however given that "Belair's battalion" had gone and rooted out every last doubt concerning the integrity of Jerome Park's racing surface, Don Cameron was now adamant about getting the show on the road. Still and all, Fannie Hertz couldn't ship in good conscious without first consulting that individual who'd actually given her Count Fleet. Happy as always to lend an ear, Mr. John D. Hertz then frankly forwarded, "I mean if you're really that worried about him dear, then have *Stan* come over and kick the tires."

Interlude - Count Fleet's Supplementary Support System

A native Czechoslovakian who'd immigrated to the United States with his family at age five, John D. Hertz made hay as both a sports reporter and a prize fighter before he assumed the role of "jockey valet" at Roby Racetrack in Indiana. Shortly fed up with performing menial chores (like scouring soiled riding effects), Hertz resultantly (and resourcefully) scraped together enough loot to launch the "Yellow Cab Company". In the sequel, Yellow Cab Co. helped finance "Hertz Rent a Car", a corporation which has remained an effectual force in global transportation for nearly a century.

Stan Martin's matte finish business card simply said, "**BLACKSMITH**" yet concerning Count Fleet's career, this one-in-a-million horseman had contributed infinitely more than just a few flathead nails. Truly a wizard when it came to band-aiding wounded equines, Martin's anatomical expertise came in especially handy after Fannie Hertz's Champion was unintentionally sideswiped by a racer (appropriately named Vindictive) in the 1943 Wood Memorial. Subsequently led into the winner's circle at Aqueduct Racetrack with a lacerated left hind hoof, Count Fleet now looked to be off the Kentucky Derby trail however with a little help from Johnny Longden, (who continuously iced his mount's massive cut inside of a train car bound for Louisville) Martin evoked just enough medicinal magic to "keep the wheels turning".

Hurrying over that same hour, Stan Martin then canvassed Count Fleet "from A to Z" before he pleasurably pronounced, "Well, I'll put it this way Mrs. Hertz. If this were a poker table, you'd be holding aces."

Though made to feel a bit better by Martin's analogy, stall #6's hesitant owner nevertheless fussed, "You know Stan, I think the reason I'm so hesitant is because I once heard Don say, 'A real clash against solid competition is much harder on a horse than any breeze could ever be.' That means his ankle might get us to the race but not necessarily through the race."

As he stepped out from behind: John D. Hertz, Johnny Longden and Mr. Sam, a plain-spoken Don Cameron candidly issued, "The "Sport of Kings" will always be fraught with danger ma'am, that's the naked truth. You have my word though, if I ever suspect through the course of training that this animal isn't totally and utterly sound, then we'll promptly revert back to "retirement mode"."

In back of lightly kissing her Champion's downy cheek, Mrs. Hertz at last surrendered, "Oh, just go ahead and send him over Don. I suppose, and my husband will attest, that all this mollycoddling is just the mother in me."

A fixture at Paradise Farms five days running, Lucien Laurin felt no less than stumped with regard to remedying his racer's ill-timed ailment. Even attempting acupuncture at one point, Penny Chenery's trusted trainer had undoubtedly served up the whole enchilada and yet, Secretariat remained bedridden with a particularly pesky pestilence. Besieged each day with thousands of get well cards, "Big Red's" celebrity status was seemingly status quo however until a clean bill of health presented itself, Jerome Park would be minus its "mane attraction".

Surreptitiously slipping into stall #9 at the hour of 5:52 AM, Lucien Laurin then proceeded to gently blindfold a certain pair of slumping eyelids. (Now made to think that day break was still a good ways off, Secretariat would thus go right on accruing the very best medicine imaginable.) Soon sealing stall #9's front door behind him, Laurin next looked to claim his own slice of essential shuteye (even if that meant hijacking a nearby hay bale).

Despite his resentment for the clanging equine transport truck which had woken him, "Big Red's" burned out conditioner remained neighborly in the company of: Robert J. Kleberg, Max Hirsch, Warren Mehrtens, Homely the mutt and one other handsome, yet unfamiliar face. After apologizing for the sudden hullabaloo, Kleberg went on to say, "Well I hate leaving you here all by your lonesome Lucien, but my guy has finally bulked up enough whereas we can breeze him. Hey and by the way, let me introduce Pastel Garcia. This here's the fella who used to break in all of King Ranch's rookies! Man and let me tell you, why during those first few months, Assault must've shed him some thirty times! Ain't that right Pastel?! Anyway, we're taking him along to Jerome Park as a sort of all-around assistant."

While pretending not to notice Warren Mehrtens' mortification, Laurin remarked, "Put 'er there Pastel, and now if you don't mind me asking, did that gnarled hoof scare you at first?"

"Scare him?!" Kleberg interrupted. "Why nothing unnerves this hombre! And frankly sir, you're looking at someone with hands like Arcaro. Alas, it's just a shame for me that the *Good Lord* made him six-foot three!"

Perceptive that a certain jockey was growing more uncomfortable by the second, Max Hirsch hence wedged it, "Uh, shouldn't we get going sir? We don't want to get mired by morning rush hour."

Happy to pick up where he had left off, Laurin literally slipped back into REM sleep right as Kleberg and company hit the highway. An active and lucid dreamer throughout his entire life, stall #9's sapped squatter therefore soon conjured up an imaginary post time rendition of Jerome Park's harrowed "chute". *(Home to an eleven-stall 14kt gold starting gate, Jerome Park's "chute" could be best described as "a tail section of supplementary straightaway". More specifically, this linear tract of land was where Heaven's Premier Horse Race would originate from.)*

Blinded to what was happening out on the oval because of a nearby neighbor's Tall Lincoln Top Hat, Laurin consequently decided to scale the Winner's Enclosures' diamond encrusted wall. Now as the field turned for home, Secretariat's advantage appeared insurmountable yet curiously, Ron Turcotte was nowhere to be found. Instead, a miniature version of Assault indwelled the saddle and to boot, the "Club Footed Comet" was attempting to bite off

"Big Red's" famous blue and white checkered hood with his front teeth!

Roused this time around by a massive rush of adrenaline, Laurin literally jumped up like a jackrabbit and then gravely muttered, "Assault is a potential stumbling stone for us."

Chapter 6 - Booking Futures

Originating just before noon on October 10th, Citation's initial jog around Jerome Park ultimately played out in front of the largest "workout crowd" that Al Snider had ever seen. Now while "Big Cy" came and went resembling a bone fide "9 to 5 shot", the exact opposite was true with regard to Warren Wright Sr.'s other entry. Continuously bolting towards and caroming off the outer rail all through his debut, "Mr. Longtail's" childlike antics eventually led one fan to scoff, "I'm sorry, but this animal is an utter disgrace to Calumet's colors! Why on his best day, Whirlaway couldn't get within five lengths of Citation!"

In the course of considering whether or not to confront the 350 lb. Spaniard who had just slandered her all-time favorite thoroughbred, *Adelphia Armour* angrily thought, *"It never fails, there's always one in every crowd."*

Interlude - The Queen Who Reigned Over
the "Sport of Kings"

Christened "Lady Long Shot" by her contemporaries, Adelphia Armour owned a reputation for prognosticating that which was unimaginable. For instance, Jerome Park's "finest" frequenter actually wound up signing a deposit slip for $25,000 the Monday after an 8-1 shot named "Upset"

90

won the 1919 Sanford Memorial Stakes (you'll remember that this is the race that haunts Johnny Loftus since it is the only blemish on Man o' War's record). Striking again inside of a damp Saratoga Race Course on Travers Day in 1930, Armour this time cleaned up to the tune of $50,000 on Jim Dandy (in case you forgot, Jim Dandy is the 100-1 shot that Willie Saunders loves to remind Earl Sande about).

A native New Yorker who'd become utterly smitten with Whirlaway (thanks to a certain $7,500 Kentucky Derby "Win Ticket"), Adelphia Armour thus found herself parked front row at Belmont Park when Calumet Farms won its first Triple Crown Championship. Sadly however, the celebration soon turned sour. See, later on that evening as she crossed 5th Avenue, "Lady Long Shot" got stuck in no man's land between a Metropolitan Cop and an armed purse snatcher. Suddenly tangled inside of a tempestuous crossfire, Armour never even felt the stray .357 caliber round that tore her heart in two.

Unable to extinguish her enmity, "Lady Long Shot" therefore bequeathed a tap on the shoulder and then gushed, "The only disgraceful entity around here sir is that mouth of yours! My Goodness, what I wouldn't do for a muzzle! You know and incidentally, are you even aware that Whirlaway's final Kentucky Derby clocking is four seconds faster than Citation's? Bah, all this nonsense about five lengths! Believe me pal; if you are willing to impart five lengths in a heads up proposition, well then your stakes are my pleasure!"

Interlude - Our Scene's Villain

To say that Salbatore Zarcos was born under a lucky star would be well, an understatement of epic proportion. See the fact was, the object of Adelphia Armour's ire had "money to burn" on account of a parental inheritance which had included 10,000 acres of coarse Canadian countryside (and besides valuable timber, this wilderness also happened to accommodate North America's largest uranium deposit). Eventually migrating to Miami, FL in 1947, Zarcos subsequently purchased several pricey thoroughbreds yet shortly thereafter, an unquenchable lust for "large-scale action" gained priority over animal husbandry.

While it took a lot to get Pomeroy J. Mandalay's attention off of his Windsor tan workout diary, a clash between "whales" was always a must-see. Now although he was initially distracted by Adelphia Armour's foxy figure, "Paradise's premier handicapper" quickly peeked up again when Salbatore Zarcos stated, "Look doll-face, I would expect Citation's Derby clocking to be a bit "pedestrian" seeing as how he ran in knee deep slop! Of course if you check out the chart, you'll find that "Big Cy" barreled over a lightning fast strip when he got to the Big Apple. Hey, you know and come to think of it, the same can be said about Whirlaway! Gee, later on tonight I think I'll go back and look up which one of Calumet's Champions owns the faster Belmont Stakes time, uh, by nearly three whole seconds!"

As she agitatedly dug one of her five inch heels down into Jerome Park's shimmering silver apron, "Lady Long Shot" snarled, "You sir, are truly loathsome! Furthermore, it's obvious that you totally underestimate Eddie Arcaro!"

"Well you're not completely mistaken ma'am." Zarcos taunted. "However, I certainly don't underestimate "The Master"! In fact, he's the only reason why Whirlaway won't finish up fifteen lengths behind Citation!"

After a long roll of the eyes, Armour flagrantly pronounced, "Ugh, can we please just finalize this contract so I can escape your repulsive presence!"

In the middle of twirling his massively waxed mustache, the apron's wealthiest soul cited, "You're not going to believe this missy, but in October of 1953, America's greatest proposition gambler also said to me, 'Your stakes are my pleasure.' And it followed that I gutted *Titanic Thompson* to the tune of $500,000! Therefore, for posterity's sake, let's make it half a million. Err, so in summary, we are heads up for $500,000 in Heaven's Premier Horse Race, Citation verses Whirlaway, and of course I'm siding with Citation minus a five length handicap."

Given that "Mr. Longtail's" first impression was worse than appalling, "Lady Long Shot" pretty much lived up to her nickname when she returned, "I consent to those terms, um, on one condition; should either half of Calumet's contingent scratch, our arrangement would then instantly become null and void."

With his typical wise guy attitude, Zarcos theatrically replied, "If that's what it will take for you to sleep at night doll, then so be it. Uh, now since I have a relative that is held in high esteem by one Leonard Walter Jerome, I'm positive that we'll be able to store our respective antes inside of the Clubhouse's fortified floor safe. After all, a wager of this size should be entirely guaranteed! Well then, shall we shake hands and make everything official?"

Once she had back peddled a few feet, Armour itemized, "I don't need to confirm my word with some inane ritual sir. Besides, the thought of touching you utterly nauseates me. You know and lastly, even though your request for a secured deposit insults my integrity, I'm in love with any arrangement that will prevent us from ever crossing paths again!"

Chapter 7 - Battle Royal

Because the entire chute was undergoing some light surface maintenance, Jerome Park's eleven-stall 14kt gold starting gate had been moved up near the three-sixteenths pole. Keeping his head turned towards the straightaway as he led Samuel D. Riddle's mounted racer down the backstretch, George Conway eventually broke the air's stillness with, "Thankfully the grounds superintendent left that contraption facing the wire like I asked."

Feeling certain that yet another fiasco was forthcoming, Charlie Kurtsiner consequently cracked, "Well yesterday I almost offered him a hundred bucks to sabotage it! Sorry boss, but every time we gate school, I feel like we're back in Louisville!"

As he reminisced about how War Admiral's unwillingness to load had delayed the start of the 1937 Kentucky Derby by eight minutes, Conway concurrently caught sight of an incoming blue and white checkered horse trailer. (Now since some scuttlebutt pertaining to Secretariat's possible emergence had recently gone viral, hundreds of news correspondents were currently camped all across Equine Chateau #9's half-acre foraging field.) Having no use for the sudden buzz that had unnerved his brown colored co-conspirator, Kurtsinger thus complained, "Pipe down you nincompoops! Gee whiz, you might think that *Pegasus* just flew in!"

In that his mount clearly saw what was forthcoming, Kurtsinger again had to play baby sitter when he arrived behind the starting gate. (One who'd witnessed War

Admiral's classic song and dance more times than he'd care to remember, Pomeroy J. Mandalay therefore turned his attention towards those other "mane-characters" that had suddenly shown up at the gap.) Controlled by their jockeys and in the clutches of their conditioners, Count Fleet and Assault now stretched out their necks before they looked at each other with identical guises which seemed to say, *"Oh, it's just War Admiral being War Admiral."*

Unlike the ultra-conservative Don Cameron (a.k.a., the trainer standing to his immediate left), Max Hirsch had unapologetically pushed the pedal to the metal. (Set to breeze for the second time in three days, Assault would now actually attempt to make amends for a disastrous debut, one that had left "Team Kleberg" down a man.)

Reasonably concerned for Pastel Garcia (because his regular rider was currently one big bruise), Hirsch for that reason cautioned, "You saw him unexpectedly ditch Warren so stay on your toes son. O.K. then like we talked about, a short warm up, then give me five-eighths in around 1:02."

While he stared at the straightaway's complimentary sideshow, Garcia concernedly pointed out, "It appears that Conway's crew is having a rough go of it sir. Mm, maybe we should wait until they're finished."

A stickler for staying on schedule, Hirsch hence rationalized, "There's plenty of room between the starting gate and the outer rail Pastel. Just corner wide off the turn and swing around them."

After he'd attended the "Club Footed Comet's" snappy takeoff, Don Cameron looked up at his jockey and directed, "Just a light lope out to the three-eighths pole and back."

Bummed because he'd been handcuffed for the third time in as many training sessions, Johnny Longden as a result thought, *"Uh, why are we restraining a racehorse who's obviously raring to go?"*

Relevant to the current backdrop, Johnny Longden wasn't the only soul who was running out of patience. Now doubling as a lead statue behind stall #1, War Admiral's abiding bullheadedness had finally made George Conway heatedly growl, "You got any suggestions there Charlie?!"

Behind producing a black bandana from out of his back pocket, Kurtsinger posed, "I bet he'll load in if we turn out the lights! Here you go boss, blindfold him with this!"

"Nah, he's too smart for that old trick!" Conway thundered. "Eh, tap his backside a few times with your whip!"

Upon seeing that a spanking wasn't the answer either, the strip's seething conditioner screamed, "Why you mutinous mongrel, I'll get you in that stall!"

Despite the fact that just one kick would spell curtains, Conway remained locked in a stalemate with War

Admiral's buttocks until Kurtsinger proposed, "What about enlisting some reinforcements sir?!"

As he dejectedly circled back around his Champion's bow, Conway puffed, "*Sampson* himself couldn't dislocate this perverse animal Charlie! You know, that does it! I'm gonna try to lead him in by the ears!"

Since he was mixed up in one of those textbook "desperate times call for desperate measures" moments, Jerome Park's only stationary jockey quipped, "I say if your health insurance is paid up, then go for it."

With ten fingers that were figuratively crossed, Conway determinedly docked War Admiral and then immediately shouted, "Amen and hallelujah, it worked Charlie!"

"We're not out of the woods yet sir!" Kurtsinger warned. "Shut those rear doors!"

Subsequent to scooting sideways past fifteen hands of slippery horseflesh, George Conway caught sight of Assault's strewn forehead blaze. Floated out some fifteen paths wide by Garcia as he entered Jerome Park's straightaway, the "Club Footed Comet" then proceeded to "thread the needle" (though not to everyone's delight). Under the impression that he'd been challenged to single combat, War Admiral thus immediately torpedoed both his unsuspecting jockey and stall #1's sealed front entrance.

Spooked by an abrupt smash and boom, Pastel Garcia accordingly took a look back over his left shoulder. Winging it now at over forty-five miles per hour, War Admiral also seemed completely bent on kindling the training season's first major catastrophe. Luckily, Garcia was somehow able to snag the runaway who would have otherwise landed square in the center of Leonard Jerome's living room!

Since War Admiral had literally spearheaded stall #1's front doors, Max Hirsch already knew that his clockwise dash around Jerome Park's clubhouse turn would end with him happening upon a colossal cranial contusion. The second bystander to arrive alongside Jerome Park's Finish Line, George Conway quickly caught his breath and then gasped, "I want you to take a good look at the Admiral Max, 'cause your face is about to resemble his!"

Honestly seeing himself as blameless, Hirsch on that account back talked, "Look George, you guys don't own the strip ya know! I mean if this donkey is gonna flip out like that, then school him when nobody else is around!"

Because he had never really been all that skilled at trading verbal jabs, Conway therefore decided to throw a literal one instead. Now in an effort to hang onto what was left of his top lip, Assault's flinty conditioner quickly countered with the type of right cross that would have made *Rocky Marciano* proud. Spared an ensuing left hook because Don Cameron had run in and shoved him out of harm's way, Conway nevertheless complained, "Stand aside man, this doesn't concern you!"

One who earnestly believed, "Blessed are the peacemakers," Pastel Garcia consequently dismounted at an angle that hindered Max Hirsch's determined advance.

Arriving on horseback seconds later, Johnny Longden then aided the "armistice effort" by parking Count Fleet right in-between Jerome Park's fuming pugilists. Ultimately mad enough to fight their way through a myriad of obstacles, Hirsch and Conway thereupon engaged in "Round 2" up until that moment when a ringing gunshot stopped everyone dead in their tracks.

Accurately fired into the oval's inner fringe, August Belmont's 7" barrel .357 caliber revolver had just served a deafening ultimatum. Forced to chase down War Admiral's and Assault's bridals (because his business partner had made like *Jesse James*), a boiling Leonard Jerome next blared, "Confine that weapon to its holster August! And as for you "gentlemen", either shake hands, or extricate yourselves from these premises, permanently!!"

In back of "burying the hatchet" and reclaiming Assault, Max Hirsch humiliatingly delivered, "Please forgive me for abusing your hospitality Mr. Jerome. Rest assured it won't happen again. C'mon Pastel, we best get going. "

After he'd likewise accepted George Conway's apology, the "King of Wall Street" beseeched, "I say Mr. Longden, can you please do me a humongous favor and check on Mr. Kurstsinger? I need to take War Admiral over to see our resident veterinarian."

Behind reaching the three-sixteenths pole courtesy of Count Fleet, Johnny Longden communicated, "I heard you hit the deck from clear across the track Charlie. You want I should go get the resident physician?"

"Negative." Kurtsinger groaned. "Ugh, I just need some ice for my shoulder."

As he slid forward in the saddle, the strip's would-be cabby urged, "Hop on then, I'll take you back to the gap."

Because his concerns went well beyond some mild bruising, Kurtsinger grilled, "How's the Admiral Johnny? Tell it to me straight now, is he hurt bad?"

While he took in stall #1's disfigured front doors, Longden laughed, "Well, he's certainly in better shape than this starting gate!"

Chapter 8 - No Greater Love...

Though he had tried "counting sheep", Steve Cauthen's attention kept drifting back towards a digital alarm clock that was set to buzz exactly one hour before Affirmed's 7:00 AM conditioning session. Now seeing as how it was situated just three blocks south of Jerome Park, Louis Wolfson's two-story vacation villa was as convenient of a headquarters as one could ask for however like a wise man once said, "Not all that glitters is gold." (The fact was that ever since he'd changed addresses, "The Kid" had continually crossed swords with a common psychological condition called "adjustment insomnia".)

In that he was determined to make the most out of a lousy situation, Cauthen suddenly shook off his king bed's beige down comforter. (See, if word on the street was true, then only forty-five minutes remained until Secretariat's highly anticipated occupational debut. Hence, here was a potential opportunity to scout the backside's top brass and even if by some chance "Big Red" was a no-show, "The Kid" knew that he would alternatively get to spend some extra quality time with Equine Chateau #11's charming lease-holder.)

Interlude - An Executive Decision

While there were certainly dangers involved with exercising over a dimly lit oval, Secretariat would nevertheless "get his feet wet" well before the cock crowed. (Why you ask?) Well, in reaction to the media's recent all-night encampment, Leonard Jerome had gone ahead with a decision to alter his acreage's hours of operation. Effective immediately, only the Connections could gain entry before the stroke of 6:00 AM and upon hearing this, Penny Chenery had proposed, "Concerning tomorrow Lucien, I'd like to finish up before the apron is made available to those ink slingers. I mean for this first go-around at least, I would rather see him train in the dark than under a microscope."

With some big-time help from some instant coffee, Steve Cauthen made it into Jerome Park's 14kt gold gated paddock right at 5:30 AM. Presently camped in a deathly quiet setting, "The Kid" therefore easily heard the gap's grey haired director say, "I estimate your visibility at around thirty yards Ronnie so for safety's sake, keep him a few paths off the rail."

Six seconds later (before either Lucien Laurin or Ron Turcotte knew what had hit him), Secretariat was scurrying past the five-eighths pole. Now in truth, "Big Red's" self-governing spirit was a huge part of what made him so darn good yet whenever she "went on record", Penny Chenery would always squeeze in, "Yes, he borders on mythical, but let me also add that, no horse is an island."

Interlude - Consigned the Keys to the Kingdom

Long before Lucien Laurin ever gave him a leg up on the latter twentieth century's most celebrated thoroughbred, Ron Turcotte worked for peanuts as a plain-old ordinary hot walker. (Hot walkers hand-walk (and thus "cool out") racehorses that have recently exercised or competed.) Becoming a full-time jockey in 1961, Turcotte actually won the 1965 Preakness Stakes on Tom Rolfein seven years before he initially bagged the Kentucky Derby and Belmont Stakes aboard Penny Chenery's own Riva Ridge. (A horse that reviled any variety of "off going", Riva Ridge's dream of a Triple Crown Championship consequently "got washed away" on a dim, dark and rainy Preakness day.)

Of course even if you were to subtract Secretariat from the equation, Ron Turcotte's name still easily belongs in Thoroughbred Horse Racing's Hall of Fame. Not only owning the highest "domestic stakes winning percentage" from 1972 to 1973, Meadow Farms' most famous rider also laid claim to the "George Woolf Memorial Jockey Award" in 1979. (This "one-time democratically given" award is presented every year to a North American thoroughbred horse racing jockey who parades exemplary character both on and off the racetrack.) Moreover, only: Ron Turcotte (1972-1973),

Jimmy Winkfield (1902-1903), Calvin Borel (2009-2010) and Victor Espinoza (2014-2015) have claimed back-to-back Kentucky Derby Championships!

Whereas the sight of Secretariat's spry locomotion was starting to poke holes in his confidence, Steve Cauthen decided to "throw it into reverse". Quick to find shed row's 10kt gold brick footpath, "The Kid" simultaneously picked up on an emphatic commotion that was set some four hundred yards in the distance. Suddenly remembering how nobody else was home when he got up, Cauthen therefore immediately took for granted that Louis Wolfson and Laz Barrera were down yonder "discussing" Affirmed's imminent seven furlong breeze.

Since he owned a glaring reputation for sleeping in, it was weird to see Gallant Fox abruptly throw open the top part of Equine Chateau #2's horizontally divided front door. At last detecting what had woken William Woodward Sr.'s narcoleptic (i.e., the smell of smoke), Steve Cauthen accordingly ditched his coffee and dashed off. Soon focused exclusively on Equine Chateau #11's fiery framework, "The Kid" as a result never saw those incoming aristocrats who were responding to Louis Wolfson's and Laz Barrera's unified cry for help.

In back of flying around the corner ahead of his business partner and flattening "The Kid" like a pancake,

Leonard Jerome shouted, "Holy smokes! You mean Affirmed is trapped in there?! Everyone quick then, follow me!"

In spite of taking a blow that would have stunned an elephant, Steve Cauthen gradually got back to his feet as: Jerome, Belmont, Wolfson and Barrera fetched "Storage Pavilion C's" fifty meter industrial hose. Now even though the backside's third auxiliary fire hydrant happened to be located in the dead center of Equine Chateau #11's foraging field, there was still one tiny little problem. Unintentionally damaged by the lawn maintenance crew, this hydrant's release lever was only good for filling Belmont's mouth with, "We need a tool that can straighten this handle!"

Following that instant where he hatched "Plan B", Steve Cauthen went and commandeered "Storage Pavilion C's" aluminum leveling rake. "Swinging for the fences" in next to no time, "The Kid" consequently made short work of Equine Chateau #11's facial bay window. Never stopping to think of the dangers that lay ahead, shed row's Good-Samaritan subsequently dove headfirst into a scene taken straight out of "Dante's Inferno".

Behind getting on his belly beneath the rising smoke, the backside's breaker and enterer proceeded to slither about and shout out his horse's name. Eventually checking in looking half-asphyxiated, Affirmed twice neighed and then grievously contorted his body in a way that conveyed, *"Better think fast Jack, 'cause I can't fit through that window you just dove through!"*

As chunks of burning debris continued to rain down all around him, Steve Cauthen clumsily threw a leg over his hard coughing Champion. Mindful that he was about to emulate *Evil Knievel,* "The Kid" therefore tensed his entire body before he applied the spurs. (Of course as luck would

108

have it, August Belmont magically fixed the backside's third auxiliary fire hydrant just as Equine Chateau #11's charred front door splintered into a million pieces.)

Despite his endeavor to sit up as Leonard Jerome's troubled face came into focus, Steve Cauthen was cautioned, "Easy does it son. This body of yours has been put through the wringer!"

While Jerome Park's resident physician continued to wipe away some lingering scalp soot with a warm wash cloth, "The Kid" whispered, "Where am I?"

Once he'd finished circling around the front of Guest Room #3's four-post canopy bed, August Belmont reassuringly said, "Safe inside the Clubhouse young man."

In the course of contemplating Cauthen's heavily bandaged right arm, the "King of Wall Street" filled in, "You must have lost consciousness just before you smashed through that door boy. Eh, we immediately hosed you down, however you still have a pretty fair size second degree burn here."

Following a slow shake of the head, Louis Wolfson intensely interjected, "Man, you came out of that barn looking like Halley's Comet! Thankfully, Affirmed didn't trample you when you belly flopped!"

After letting go of a weak cough, Cauthen grunted, "Affirmed; where is he?"

With a tone that was now much more relaxed, Wolfson informed, "He's chilling out inside of Equine Chateau #10. Laz had to dress a few minor abrasions but otherwise, he's no worse for the wear."

"But unfortunately Mr. Cauthen, you are." Jerome sighed. "And since that arm will require regular attention, you'll remain a guest of this Clubhouse until further notice. Be encouraged though sir, for uh, *Doctor Luke* here lists you as "probable" for our little year-end extravaganza. Now if you'll excuse me, I must go rejoin the Fire Marshal. See, he believes this morning's blaze was sparked by a faulty fuse and so, off we go on a four hour property wide inspection."

As his remaining guests softly chatted amongst themselves, Steve Cauthen enthusiastically took back up with the Sandman. Delicately stirred by the upstairs butler at exactly 6:00 PM, the "King of Wall Street's" new house guest thereafter became the gracious recipient of both a dinner tray and the Eternity Times' evening edition. Completely famished, "The Kid" thus instantly honed in on his 24 oz. bone-in rib-eye steak rather than a bold headline which read, "**Horse Racing Nation Dubs Cauthen a Hero!!!**"

Chapter 9 - The Point of No Return

In back of coming to fundamental terms with "Wise Men Web Developers", Leonard Jerome called the Eternity Times' breaking news hotline and relayed, "Please inform your readers that tickets for Heaven's Premier Horse Race will be made available at 12:01 PM on November 15th via the web at www.Heaven'sPremierHorseRace/Tickets.com."

Three days later, as he jellied a cheese filled breakfast blintz out on his Clubhouse's veranda, the "King of Wall Street" aired, "When I turned on my phone this morning there was a text from one of our web developers August. He asked if we could get a ticket price guide over to him by 2:00 PM."

As he passed his HD tablet over the table, Belmont imparted, "I am way ahead of you chap. Here, I've electronically inscribed ninety-eight ascending admission rates onto an architectural sketch of the Main Grandstand. Um, so it's my opinion that $1000 is fair for those second level nosebleed seats in Sections: 2W, 2X, 2Y and 2Z, however I'm thinking that I might have undervalued Section 2B. After all, that zone is right on the finish line directly behind the Luxury Tenements and Owners' Boxes."

Once he had scanned the presented screen, Jerome stated, "You know, given the product we're offering, this menu is totally justified sir. Yet, seeing as how we are both well, filthy stinking rich, let's bless Horse Racing Nation by scaling these rates back a tad. Say by, fifty percent."

"You must be off your rocker!" Belmont blasted. "Why, if we do that, we'll leave a king's ransom on the table!"

"We'll lose nearly a quarter of it to taxes anyway." Jerome shrugged. "Uh, and now instead of squabbling over small potatoes, let's actually discuss a matter that has real consequence. I mean, here it is November 14th and we don't even have a basic outline yet for December 30th's Transcendental Gala Dinner!"

Because his mind was on money rather than merriment, Belmont sarcastically chattered, "You know, you're right Leonard. Heck, what's five billion dollars anyway? In fact, why stop at fifty percent?! Why, I say we go all the way and let Horse Racing Nation waltz in here free of charge!"

Since this had been his heart's desire from the very beginning, the "King of Wall Street" wasted no time smirking, "As you wish August."

In the wake of being notified (by one of his trusted media moles) that the Eternity Times' evening edition headline would read, "**Gratis Tickets for Heaven's Premier Horse Race Sell Out in Two Minutes!!!**" Leonard Jerome fetched a bottle of Louis Roederer Cristal Brut Champagne from his bedroom's wall mounted mini-bar. Before a cork characterized "2005" could be cleared for takeoff however, the upstairs butler appeared and informed, "Pardon the interruption sir, but Mr. Belmont is on line one."

Now although he truly expected to hear something along the lines of, "Congratulations old boy!" the "King of Wall Street" instead abruptly took in, "Um, are you aware that the ticketing website's standby list contains over three hundred thousand names?!"

Determined to let nothing take the wind out of his sails, Jerome hence contended, "Rules are rules August. And by order of the Fire Marshal, the Main Grandstand's maximum occupancy is two hundred thousand saints. I mean, I agree that the website's surplus is unfortunate, but c'mon, it was to be expected."

Courtesy of a brain that was moving at a million miles per hour, Belmont suddenly buzzed, "I knew it! I knew we had too small of an arena! It's o.k. though because do you know what we're going to do? We're going to install three hundred thousand new seats! And don't worry old boy, I'm going to finance the construction with my own capital!"

"Whoa, back up a minute." Jerome snorted. "Err, construction of what?"

"Why, temporary bleachers of course!" Belmont boomed. "We'll encase the entire oval, lest of course those areas which are taken up by the: Main Grandstand, Clubhouse, paddock and gap!"

Since he was well acquainted with large-scale building projects (i.e., his own racetrack) the "King of Wall Street" rationalized, "Look August, even if you had the entire Army Corps of Engineers at your disposal, forty-six days is simply not enough time to complete such a massive undertaking!"

Bound and determined, Belmont thus cried, "You know, here I am trying to follow your philanthropic example and yet you're doing everything in your power to try and discourage me! I mean, at least let me call up a few contractors to see if they think this is possible!"

Ultimately recycling those words that had become oh so famous, Jerome at long last sighed, "As you wish August."

Despite being squeezed on all sides like a canned sardine, Pomeroy J. Mandalay still managed to get a half-way decent look at Seattle Slew's sizzling six furlong breeze. Consequent to climbing his way up to Section 2W, "Paradise's premier handicapper" cracked open his Windsor Tan Workout Diary and wrote,

Mid-Term Rankings

11. **Sir Barton** - Came back lame from his initial gallop and has done very little since. Can't even walk shed row without grimacing and vehemently detests every piece of metal that Ethan Bishop forges. All told, Ross' unshod equine remains this contest's prohibitive outsider.

10. **Whirlaway** - Because they are dealing with the worst kind of eccentric, "Mr. Longtail's" handlers have already accumulated their fair share of grey hairs. Despite his custom "right side only" blinkered hood (and Eddie Arcaro's very best efforts), this one

still invariably bolts towards the outer fence at the beginning of every workout. Retaining faith that he can fix things via a tried and true adaptation scheme, Ben Jones thus spends countless hours walking his brat directly aside Jerome Park's inner rail.

9. **Count Fleet** - Appears sound but has only been allowed to jog. Quite obviously, Don Cameron has reservations about pressuring his Champion's suspect left-front ankle.

8. **Affirmed** - Given that he was almost reduced to a pile of ashes, this one is blessed to even be in the conversation. Now aside from a "so-so" seven weeks, another point at issue here is that (due to Steve Cauthen's scorched arm) some "average Joe" will be breezing Louis Wolfson's battler for the foreseeable future. In a camp where chemistry is everything, this is hardly a recipe for success.

7. **Assault** - Another middling contestant who is minus his regular rider. Victimized by lower back spasms and Sciatic nerve pain since being unseated last month, Warren Mehrtens' return date is still up in the air.

6. **Omaha** - If he persists with this "mano a mano" philosophy, James Fitzsimmons might inadvertently break the "Belair Bullet's" spirit. Though always able to save face, Omaha is nevertheless a collective 0 for 10 vs. his father. Still, this one's sheer immensity will come in handy should things get physical when the gates open.

5. **Gallant Fox** - Although he brings his "A-Game" every time out, three long-established bad habits bear mentioning: 1) Clinically co-dependent, the "Fox of Belair" often crowds those horses he spars against, Omaha included. 2) Lately when he blows

116

past a workhorse, Belair's best hope celebrates (and consequently decelerates). 3) A habitual "stargazer" to begin with, Earl Sande's sidekick has recently "thrown another log on the fire" (in the form of a pre-occupation with those pennants that are atop Jerome Park's Main Grandstand).

4. **War Admiral** - Following his camp's melee with Robert J. Kleberg's crew, Charlie Kurtsinger tried to make light of everything by joking, "Not even a locked 14kt gold barricade can slow our horse down!" Naturally said in fun, Kurtsinger's statement nevertheless accurately depicts how well Samuel D. Riddle's gutty racer has trained. If this one draws a good post position and agrees to load in, a gate to wire performance is not inconceivable.

3. **Seattle Slew** - Shines brighter and brighter with each succeeding breeze; undoubtedly, the "value play" in here.

2. **Citation** - Outruns the wind, is totally unflappable and is ridden by a soul who desperately seeks redemption. For sure, "Big Cy" has Penny Chenery's attention.

1. **Secretariat** - Don't look now but, "Big Red" has gone from sick to sensational in just three weeks time. It's scary to think that he's just gotten started. A deserving favorite and the horse to beat come December 31st.

On the heels of supplementing his diary, Pomeroy J. Mandalay mused over a topography that was now devoid of:

horses, horsemen and horseplayers. Eventually influenced by the sight of Jerome Park's titanic tote board, "Paradise's premier handicapper" first juggled some numbers and then jotted down, *"Liquidation of Paradise Petroleum Inc. stock will boost bankroll to $300,000."*

Chapter 10 - Trading Places

Even though he was remotely stationed behind the far turn's outer rail, Salbatore Zarcos still let out an appreciative whistle as Al Snider jogged Citation back through the gap. Now because Horse Racing Nation had just witnessed the season's fastest five furlong breeze, you could literally cut the electricity inside of Leonard Jerome's empire with a knife. That being said, after he heard an acquaintance on the apron arrogantly shout, "Secretariat who?!" Zarcos sourly sighed, "Dale you dimwit, I told you who the best horse was eight weeks ago."

Soon seized by a wee withdrawal symptom, Jerome Park's most opinionated Spaniard resultantly pulled out some cigarette papers and a large purple pouch of loose tobacco. Quick to stick a gram of rolled up shredded leaf between his teeth, "Big Cy's" biggest fan then finalized things with help from a "strike anywhere match" and a nearby raised sprinkler head.

For the reason that Citation was the day's one and only worker, Salbatore Zarcos next got to thinking about lunch. An ambitious eater (to say the least), Adelphia Armour's noted antagonist therefore suddenly pictured both an extra-large meat lover's pizza, and that which existed in the basement of "Sal's Mid-Town Italian Café". (Namely, an eighteenth century style underground faro game.)

Beckoned from out of the blue as he began to depart, Zarcos thereupon twisted his neck around until it lined up with one Al Snider. Standing there holding a Dominican Double Corona Cigar, Citation's dust spattered jockey tarried for a few seconds before he patiently repeated, "Say mister, you got a light?"

Though nearly paralyzed with surprise, Zarcos nonetheless furnished a blue flame and then gushed, "Gosh that workout, it gave me goose-bumps!"

In back of retreating and blowing an ashen smoke ring, Snider offhandedly uttered, "Mm, you don't say."

As he looked out across the oval, the far turn's accommodator asseverated, "Cross my heart! But where are my manners señor, my name is..."

"Salbatore Zarcos." Snider interrupted. "See friend, word travels fast when somebody antes up half a million bucks. Uh, and with reference to your wager, please refrain from roasting me for all of eternity. You know, should you happen to lose."

After taking a short drag off of his cigarette, Zarcos genially returned, "Ah, that's never been my style sir, although, I can't speak for the rest of Horse Racing Nation. Uh, what I'm saying is that gamblers, especially horseplayers, don't always lose with grace!"

Because he possessed a thousand "tales from the trenches", Snider suddenly jumped in with, "Speaking of, here's one for the age's partner. Picture it, the ninth and final at Hialeah, and I'm paired with this 75-1 shot who isn't fit to pull an Italian ice wagon. Anyway, we're thirty lengths back at the three-eighths pole so instead of senselessly hitting this mule, I lay aside my whip and just skate through the lane. Now a few minutes later while I'm dismounting, this disgruntled rail-bird starts howling about how I stiffed his horse. Next thing I know, a size thirteen shoe is flying straight towards my head!"

Once he had wiped the disgust off of his face, Paradise's most pompous punter pronounced, "What a classless pig! Did you give him the old "one-two"?!"

"That would not have been prudent on my part." Citation's jockey certified. "See, my brother-in-law is an ex-Green Beret!"

While chuckling, Zarcos contended, "Well hey, you can make everything up to him and more in about six weeks eh?!"

With a reserved inflection, Snider related, "Well I'll admit Salbatore, I wouldn't trade places with anyone, not even Turcotte. And believe you me, I totally realize how different life would be had Arcaro not renounced his right to ride "Big Cy"!"

Born with absolutely no "filter", the far turn's weighty wise guy therefore carelessly yakked, "Yes, strange how Mr. Wright didn't try to persuade him otherwise."

First forsaking his next Dominican flavored draw, Snider then sorely posed, "Oh, so you're saying you would have?"

"Well, conventional wisdom says, 'pair the superior jockey with the superior horse.'" Zarcos overbearingly lipped. "But hey, it's all a moot point anyway as far as I'm concerned. I mean the way it stands; Citation could whip Whirlaway by five lengths with yours truly in the saddle!"

Of the belief that his acquaintance's cute little "conventional wisdom comment" had been highly un-called for, Citation's ruffled rider thus reciprocated, "Yeah well, I hate to break it to you butterball, but they don't make a racing saddle big enough for your behind!"

Instead of retaliating with a cheap shot of his own, Zarcos confidently crowed, "Hey, go ahead and poke fun all you want son! It's all good 'cause at day's end, you're gonna help me win half a million bucks whether you like it or not!"

As he tempestuously trampled his cigar underfoot, Snider sternly promised, "Fat chance of that Salbatore! Uh, no pun intended!"

While he kept close tabs on his hungry horse (who was literally buried up to his eyes in oats) Jimmy Jones simultaneously dealt out the afternoon's sixth hand of gin rummy. Seated on the other side of Equine Chateau #8's mahogany tripod table, Ben Jones was currently dishing out a beating yet the exact opposite was true with reference to the game which mattered most. No longer able to concentrate, Calumet's senior conditioner consequently threw down his cards and then communicated, "So I didn't say anything right of the bat because you were brimming about Citation's breeze but the truth is, well, I had a conference call with Mr. Wright and Arcaro early this morning. Doggone it, all of Horse Racing Nation is gonna be heartbroken but there is just no other choice. Whirlaway has to be scratched."

"Scratched?! Please tell me you're kidding!" Jimmy Jones lamented. "O.K., hey I get it, he's been a handful, but you don't understand Pop! Sending out a partial field defeats the entire purpose of this race!"

"No, you don't understand!" Ben Jones blared. "That ninny won't keep a straight line! Why over the course of a ten furlong route, he would impede half the field!"

Now just as Jimmy Jones began to say, "There must be some way," Al Snider stormed through Equine Chateau #8's single hinged side door. Thrown into a tizzy by this startling intrusion, Citation hence required some corralling by one Ben Jones who concurrently screamed, "You'd better scram before I crack your skull open boy!"

Because he didn't want to see blood get all over Equine Chateau's #8's brand new memory foam floor, Jimmy Jones quickly showed his jockey the door. "Pops" soon took up pursuit however and when he saw that his stalker indeed meant business, Snider sang out, "I'm sorry Ben, I'm sorry!! I should have knocked first!!"

Since he knew that "sorry" wasn't going to cut it, Jimmy Jones physically interfered with his father's ominous advance ahead of ordering, "Calm down before you do something you'll regret Dad! Now let's all just head back inside, I'll make some coffee."

Subsequent to sitting down beside his antagonist, Ben Jones buffaloed, "Running in here like a lunatic. You'd better have a good excuse there junior!"

As Jimmy Jones continued to prep Equine Chateau #8's Neapolitan Percolator, Snider stated, "I was in the mood for a cigar after Citation's breeze right, so I ask this fella standing near the far turn for a light. Low and behold, it turns out to be Salbatore Zarcos! You know, that Spaniard who made the half million dollar proposition bet with Adelphia Armour?"

Set off by the word "bet", Ben Jones as a result seethed, "When you realized it was him, why didn't you cut

124

out?! I mean you know that Mr. Wright doesn't want us rubbing elbows with the railbirds!"

"He was just getting a light Dad." Jimmy Jones maintained. "C'mon Al, continue."

With his next breath, Snider elaborated, "At first see, we just sort of shot the breeze. However, after I acknowledged Arcaro's altruism regarding Citation, that cob roller actually questioned Mr. Wright's decision not to intervene and, 'pair the superior jockey with the superior horse'. Huh, imagine the gall of this guy!"

Once he had read between the lines, Equine Chateau #8's elder statesman steamed, "Ah ha! So that's why you busted in here like a bedlamite! Zarcos "disrespected" you, so now you're bent on wrecking the bet he has with Armour! Well, I've got news for you pal. You can forget about teaming up with "Mr. Longtail" because he ain't gonna run! No sir! In fact by this time tomorrow, that fruitcake will be riding the rails back to Paradise Farms!"

Seeing as how he was the type who could "sell snow to an Eskimo", Whirlaway's would be pilot wisely revamped his approach and then pitched, "Look Ben, just take Zarcos out of the equation for a second. Now look, does it make sense to scratch your horse when you haven't even tried the oldest trick in the book?! Hey be honest, how many unruly racers have you seen come around under a fresh set of hands?! Hundreds right?! Man what have you got to lose?! Tell him, will ya Jimmy?!"

In that he was repulsed by the thought of a ten horse field, Citation's conditioner quietly committed, "You have to admit, he makes good sense Pop."

"I don't believe this, betrayed by my own flesh and blood!" Ben Jones bewailed. "Uh, aren't you forgetting something though fellas? Like how we're contractually bound by those riding assignments that are listed on the Charter of Competition!"

As he moved to pour three cups of coffee, Jimmy Jones maintained, "Well, where does it say that the Charter can't be amended? With that said though, I think we should garner the support of both Jerome and Belmont before we call for a vote. See, they'll naturally favor any measure that'll help preserve a full field and considering all the generosity they've shown, our fellow Connections might therefore think twice before they go and shoot this motion down."

In that he highly honored his absent superior, Ben Jones promptly insisted, "Listen boys; no one is talking to anyone until we run this entire scheme past Mr. Wright!"

Rarin' to get the ball rolling, Al Snider accordingly scampered towards Equine Chateau #8's single hinged side door while he pledged, "Don't worry Ben; I'll call him on my way to the Clubhouse."

Ironically, the 14kt gold rotary phone sitting on Leonard Jerome's upstairs' office desk started to ring right as August Belmont walked in with a rolled up blueprint that was titled, "**Temporary Bleacher Thumbnail - Real Steel Construction Company**". In back of hearing his downstairs butler explain how Al Snider had come requesting a conference, the "King of Wall Street" graciously instructed,

"Seat him in the solarium Horace, we'll be down in about twenty minutes. Oh, and please brew some tea. Yes, I think a piping hot pot of Darjeeling will do quite nicely."

Loose throughout the moment of truth thanks to some supplementary rehearsal time, Al Snider nevertheless got a weird feeling after he closed with, "So you see, even though this switch could go a long way towards preventing the aforementioned scratch; that confounded Charter of Competition has got us hogtied. I mean sure, we could write out an amendment, organize a vote and hope for the best. However, if the Connections knew that both you gentlemen were well, in our corner, it could make all the difference."

As he meticulously stirred two drops of fresh lemon juice into the contents of his bone china tea cup, Leonard Jerome staidly came out with, "You know, I've grown accustom to sipping a brunch time Bloody Mary out on my veranda Mr. Snider. Uh, and on account of this daily ritual, I accidentally attended a certain conversation today, one which, appeared to end on a rather sour note."

While his heart hastily passed over into "palpitation mode", Snider apprehensively sputtered, "You, you did?"

"Yes, I did." Jerome dryly replied. "And that sir is why the fourteen letters which spell "ulterior motive" come to mind. See, Salbatore Zarcos, that peacock, is no stranger to me. Thus, I'm guessing he somehow slighted you and now you're err dare I say 'trying to do the right thing for the wrong reason'."

The result of having his "mail read", the solarium's sojourner recoiled and then irritably said, "Peacock, now that's hitting the nail on the head."

Upon realizing that his comparison was a popular one, the "King of Wall Street" expounded, "Mm, prouder than three of them put together actually! Shoot, I rediscovered that when he showed up here a few weeks ago, uh unannounced mind you, seeking a financial trustee. Ha, believe me; the only reason why I'm the acting custodian over Paradise's preeminent proposition wager is because Zarcos' great uncle, one *Pastor Cachi Consuelos*, faithfully served as Jerome Park's chaplain from 1867 to 1874."

Because he wanted to get back to the big picture, Belmont respectfully inserted, "Ahem, if I may gentlemen. Look, ulterior motive or not, what's important here is having a complete eleven horse field come year's end! What confuses me though Mr. Snider, is why you think that you need our influence? What I'm saying is; none of your peers want to see a watered down version of this race. I'm telling you, if Whirlaway's participation can perhaps be preserved by this proposed switch, why then the Connections will gladly give the go-ahead."

Though he rarely found himself at variance with his business partner, Jerome nevertheless contradicted, "What you're not figuring into the equation August is the fact that even if everyone else does, Mr. Eddie Arcaro will never, and I mean never, go along with this whole deal. Especially after the way he publicly ceded Citation! I'm telling you, once "The Master" gives his word, that's it! There's no way he switches mounts! Nope! Not in a million years!"

"Well here's hoping that Mr. Belmont is right and you're wrong sir." Snider dejectedly sighed. "I'll also say that in light of this conversation, I definitely know where I'm headed once I finish my tea."

128

Although he had traveled to the outskirts of town and had shut off his cell phone, Eddie Arcaro was about to cross paths with yet another concerned co-worker. Presently pre-occupied with teeing up a pockmarked range-ball, "The Master" was on that account "delayed in his reaction" when he suddenly heard, "Hey champ, have you got a minute?"

Once he had picked up a splintered tee (so he could clean the grooves of his titanium head five-iron), Arcaro aired, "Wow, first Mr. Wright and now you. Shoot, I guess it is true. I did tell y'all that I'm a regular here!"

Upon discovering that Calumet's head honcho had already paid a visit to "King David's Double-Decker Driving Range", Al Snider asked, "Wait a second, Mr. Wright swung by here?"

In back of lacing one right down the middle, "The Master" enlightened, "Left about ten minutes ago. Say, the boss man mentioned it, but remind me again. At what point did I divulge that I typically spend afternoons here to unwind?"

Before he could chatter, "You mentioned it over dinner, Sunday before last," tee box #13's succeeding caller was broadsided with, "Know what? Never mind Al, it isn't important. Just know this, Wright already told me what you proposed to Ben. Oh yeah, and about how you paid Jerome and Belmont a visit."

"In hindsight, I wish I would've done things differently." Snider grieved. "In fact to be honest, right now

I'm entirely convicted that I've done our friendship a gross disservice. What I mean is; I just should have talked with you right from the get-go. Ugh, Zarcos just had me so riled up that I guess I wasn't thinking straight."

Clearly puzzled, Arcaro hence fished, "Zarcos? What's his big behind got to do with all this?"

So he could lay his head down with a clear conscience, Snider went and confided, "Truthfully Eddie, that heifer is the reason I sought Ben out in the first place. See, he said something to me today that kind of rubbed me the wrong way and well, I wouldn't mind seeing a few zeros trimmed off his bank account."

After he'd nonchalantly dismissed both his chum's confession and another range-ball, "The Master" passed along, "Here's the meat of the matter Al. Though it took awhile, I was able to convince Mr. Wright that Belmont is indeed correct. You know, about how the Connections will gladly give the go-ahead to us exchanging equines if that's the only way to perhaps preserve Whirlaway's participation. Then I told him to just have his secretary type up an amendment that everyone can sign. Yep, guaranteed amigo, by this time tomorrow, that flake housed in Equine Chateau #5 will be your problem."

Feeling like he'd fallen a bit behind, Snider thus rubbed his temples and then ranted, "But how do you know Belmont said that the Connections will gladly give the go-ahe…? Hey, wait a second! So, you're cool with us swapping mounts?!"

"I'll start by answering your first question." Arcaro grinned. "What happened was; Belmont sent Mr. Wright a text immediately after you left the Clubhouse. That's why he stopped by here. Now this isn't word for word but it basically said, '*I talked with Snider about the whole switching mounts thing and assured him that the Connections will gladly give the go-ahead. (Therefore, I'm staying out of it.) And FYI, Leonard doesn't think that "The Master" will get on board but I guarantee otherwise. If you want some peace of mind though, go and talk to him.'*"

Cut off as he started to open his mouth, Snider next ingested, "See, after Wright read me that text I immediately said, 'Everything Mr. Belmont wrote is dead on sir.' Heck, c'mon Al let's face it, I can't get Ben's long-tailed critter to listen! So, though it means going back on what I said at the Connections' Summit, I must now humbly step aside and let you "take your at bat". However, do me one favor will you? Don't climb on board Whirlaway just so you can attempt to even the score with Zarcos. I mean if asked, I want to say that you acted sacrificially in order to preserve the integrity of Heaven's Premier Horse Race."

Behind promising that he would do his best to "turn the other cheek", Snider admitted, "Well, this all went a lot smoother than I expected. I'm telling you bro, Jerome had me worried. I mean especially after the way he hollered, '*There's no way he switches mounts! Nope! Not in a million years!*'"

Following a light laugh that was aimed at his pal's admitted paranoia, Arcaro assured, "Ah, you shouldn't have worried yourself man. Jerome's obviously been dead wrong numerous times before."

Again at a loss, Snider on that account extended, "Mm, come again?"

As he yanked a fairway wood out of his Slazenger golf bag, "The Master" elucidated, "Think about it Al. If Jerome got rich playing the stock market on more than one occasion, then it makes sense that he also got taken to the cleaners on more than one occasion!"

Chapter 11 - Equine Infidelity

To be honest, not everyone was thrilled that the official digital "Post-time Countdown" on Jerome Park's tote board currently read, "**30 days - 10 hours - 41 minutes - 9 seconds**". Now though he was definitely one of those horsemen who needed something to smile about, a late running H.G. Bedwell certainly wasn't going to find his "land of milk and honey" inside of Equine Chateau #1. On the contrary, the forthcoming scene starring: Sir Barton, Johnny Loftus, Toots Thompson and Ethan Bishop would nearly move the backside's iciest trainer to tears.

The truth was that even with seventy-two years of Earthly racetrack experience under his belt (eight of those coming at Jerome Park); Ethan Bishop had just never seen anything quite like Sir Barton's ultra-sensitive hooves. Yet, in his fifteenth trip back to the drawing board, the "King of Wall Street's" brainy blacksmith had come up with an "extra-thin shock absorbing shoe" that required only three teensy nails. Confused therefore why his ill-humored horse was still completely barefoot, Bedwell consequently came through the door with, "Ugh! Come come Ethan, now what's the problem?!"

As he paraded an incredibly petite "pin spike", Jerome Park's frustrated ferrier huffed, "In all my years, I've never met a racer with more delicate feet! I mean look! This custom skewer isn't even half an inch long and still, he wants no part of it! Starts kicking the very second I implement any pressure! Toots here will tell ya! Why I almost lost my front teeth just before you walked in!"

Unable to stomach yet another setback, Bedwell resultantly flung his brown derby across the room and then roared, "Ethan please, our situation is dire! I mean you're looking at a horse who hasn't logged a single workout! Now you're not going anywhere until this animal is suitably shod!"

"He flips out the second he feels the nail!" Bishop cried. "Uh, just what do you expect me to do Harvey?!"

Because his back was square against the wall, Sir Barton's trainer turbulently beseeched, "You're supposedly the best aren't you?! Then improvise man! Heck I don't know, concoct some sort of glue!"

Again the "bearer of bad news", Equine Chateau #1's cobbler thus glanced to the side as he regretfully replied, "Unfortunately, Mr. Jerome has banned the use of adhesives for this contest. Says he's seen way too many "stick on shoes" fly off and injure those racing further back in the pack."

Rather than take no for an answer, Bedwell pressed, "C'mon man, are you trying to tell me that with today's technology, there isn't an adhesive out there that can infallibly attach four lousy horseshoes?!"

Since he sincerely ached for those pitiful faces that were staring at him, Bishop mercifully spit out, "Well, there actually is a sure fire glue that I'm familiar with. And I do have the ingredients necessary to whip up a batch, but I hope you're not in a hurry because it takes around two hours or so to cook."

"Considering I've already lost two months, what's another two hours?" Bedwell murmured. "Uh look, just get cracking on this venture Ethan. Meanwhile, I'm gonna get on the horn and see if I can get Mr. Jerome to stop by for a few minutes."

Because of H.G. Bedwell's gutsy decision to end a certain late night phone conversation with, "I guarantee he will breeze tomorrow morning sir," Commander J.K.L. Ross had been waiting with baited breath inside of Section 2W since 6:45 AM. Cloaked in a freshly pressed navel uniform that perfectly reflected daybreak's burnt orange illumination, Sir Barton's patient owner now put an eye on the proximate army of artisans who were hard at work building Heaven's biggest belt of temporary bleachers. (All with at least ten years experience, the seventy-nine soul detachment sent over from Real Steel Construction Co. had actually been laboring round-the-clock in an effort to augment Jerome Park's total capacity by one hundred and fifty percent.)

Led out to the gap by Don Cameron at half past seven, Count Fleet was that thing which ultimately stripped Ross' attention away from August Belmont's 1.5 million dollar building project. Now behind orchestrating yet another easy gallop that was put to bed about twenty yards from the gap, Johnny Longden took in, "Come down and take hold of his bridle boy! Don't be lax about it either! If he gets loose Mrs. Hertz will have both our heads!"

In back of rubbing eyeballs with an equine who obviously wanted to rip off a few furlongs, Longden babbled, "Doggone it Don, I don't understand why we're not, I mean at least let him... Aw heck, never mind."

While he worked to unfasten his Champion's saddle belt, Cameron complained, "Quit wavering and just spit it out boy!"

Though positive he was about to pry open Pandora's Box, the gap's grumbler nevertheless poured out, "Fine. What I want to know is; what gives with this ridiculous training regiment?! I mean I know you're scared he's gonna reinjure that ankle however if we're serious about winning, it's time to rev up the RPMs a little!"

After he'd heisted his horse's bridal, Cameron clamored, "Know what boy, I promised myself that I would never go down this road but since you insist on "poking the bear" let's finally get everything out in the open. So uh, do the names *Fairy Manhurst* and *Deseronto* ring-a-bell?! C'mon Johnny you remember, they were those two crème puffs that we faced in the Belmont Stakes. Gosh, weren't their odds like 28-1 and 52-1 respectively? And by the time you hit the three-eighths pole they were both back a country mile, but did you proceed to downshift? No, of course not! Instead, you let a horse that had just wretched his ankle score by twenty-five lengths! You know, an ounce of prevention in that instance probably would've saved this animal's career! Moreover, I wouldn't presently have to deal with this all encompassing fear that he's gonna break down out here!"

Believing he'd been unfairly "thrown under the bus", Longden thus shot back, "You're actually gonna stand there and blame me for what happened in the Belmont?! Dude, how could I have possibly known that he'd wrenched his ankle coming away from the barrier?! Nothing about his gait felt unusual! Oh and for the record, he dragged me down the lane, not the other way around! Huh, know what your

137

problem is Don?! You've let all of Mrs. Hertz's unwarranted apprehension rub off on you! He's one hundred percent sound do you hear me?! Man, even Stan said it! Now we can still salvage this thing but only if you stop treating him like he's made out of glass!"

As he led Count Fleet away from the oval, Cameron calmly called back, "Uh, I'm leaving before we go down the same road as Hirsch and Conway. Word to the wise though Johnny; don't tell me my business concerning this horse ever again."

Kicking a mound of dirt towards the inner rail as he did a "one-eighty", Longden subsequently muttered, "Fine man, whatever. When we get whipped though; don't come crying to me."

Rather than sulk about how Sir Barton was nowhere in sight, Commander J.K.L Ross purposely lost himself between the margins of "Act II". Climatically sailing through an 8:00 AM six furlong breeze like he had a firework tied to his fanny, Secretariat consequently made Section 2W's practical tenant sigh, "Well, they say if you can't beat 'em…"

Off the pace of presuming (around the hour of 10:00 AM) that his Champion was destined to be a no-show, Commander J.K.L. Ross slowly made his way down towards Jerome Park's sparsely populated apron. Now because he'd already pretty much put his game plan together, Ross broke out a broad grin when he caught sight of one Pomeroy J.

Mandalay. Literally "just what the doctor had ordered" that soul who was often identified as "Paradise's premier handicapper" hence instantly took in, "Mm, looks like it's about time for a new notebook."

Given that he was reviewing his workout diary's hindmost page (a.k.a., those notes tied to "Big Red's" breathtaking breeze), Mandalay went and purposely turned a cold shoulder to the air's unfamiliar voice. Undaunted by his initial failure to break the ice, Sir Barton's backslid owner therefore extended a firm hand before he formally intruded, "If you'd do me the honor sir, my name is Ross, Commander John Kenneth Leveson Ross."

Feeling like a fool in that moment where he looked up, "Paradise's premier handicapper" then turned a bright shade of red as he faintly said, "Oh, I wish I was dead; ugh, Pomeroy J. Mandalay here sir, at your service."

With a tongue that really felt like saying, "*Mm, one can only hope*," Ross casually chatted, "So I was just commenting that it looks as though another tree will soon have to make the ultimate sacrifice! Gee whiz, and considering the number of pages in that book, it's obvious that you place a tremendous amount of importance on these morning maneuvers."

Resolved at this point to remain an enigma, Mandalay for that reason misrepresented, "Actually Commander, I'm of the mind that it's extremely dangerous to assume that any given breeze, no matter how spirited, will be duplicated once the flag drops."

"Ha, yours is a predictable reply." Ross ceded. "Nevertheless, if Secretariat even manages to summon just half of his latest effort come New Year's Eve, well then the best everyone else can hope for is a silver medal."

As he made a serious face, the apron's penman heartened, "Come now Commander, you just can't automatically hand over this race! O.K. granted; your camp has encountered its fair share of obstacles. Keep in mind however that your Champion's spirit is suffused with a most telling brand of tenacity!"

Once he'd mimicked his "mark's" sober guise, Sir Barton's master sorrowfully said, "Tenacious he is sir. However, heart can only coax crippled hooves so far."

"Aw have faith." Mandalay petitioned. "Lifting enfeebled equines off the mat is Bedwell's specialty."

Throughout a prolonged head shake, Ross replied, "No amount of knowhow can rejuvenate permanently fatigued tissue Pomeroy. Alas, Sir Barton's participation, assuming he does start, will be purely ceremonial. Gosh what a colossal disappointment. I was so looking forward to backing him at a massive price."

"Backing him?" Mandalay gasped, "You mean, with money? Hold on a second. I didn't think that the Connections were allowed to tie in with the pari-mutual pools."

In what was a smart move on his part, Ross slowly led his "prey" into the Main Grandstand's west maintenance corridor before he cut loose with, "Ah, much better, can't be too careful you know. Anyway, yes you are correct sir. The Connections are one hundred percent prohibited from wagering on Heaven's Premier Horse Race. And frankly, that is why I need someone who has a reputation for staking substantial sums of cash."

On account of opening his mouth before he had put two and two together, Mandalay wound up stuttering, "Eh, but if you're not going to bet on Sir Barton, then why do you

140

need, hey, hold on a second! Oh no! You can't be aiming to, you're, you're actually going to bet on Secretariat?!"

"Pipe down will you please!" Ross implored. "There are still a few stragglers rummaging around on the apron."

While his mind continued to process a startling reality, "Paradise's premier handicapper" popped off, "But sir, take a stand against your own colors?! Why if word of such a thing ever got out, yours would be a most despised name!"

In the middle of rolling his eyes, Jerome Park's turncoat made clear, "Look man, I didn't drag you in here so we could engage in an ethical debate. Rather, I'd like to extend an extremely generous business proposition."

"Mm, well then I guess I'm all ears." Mandalay rasped. "However, it doesn't take a rocket scientist to figure out where this conversation is headed."

Taking a pinch of snuff before he got down to the nitty-gritty, Ross thus sniffled while he expounded, "Well here's another tidbit that's rather obvious sir; you are one of the select few that I can actually work through. I mean c'mon, the spectacle of some "ordinary Joe" making a seven figure wager would attract way too much attention. On the contrary, nobody bats an eye when someone with your reputation plops down a fortune! So anyway here's the deal, come year end, you'll bet one million dollars on "Big Red" for me. If he wins, I'll fork over 10% of my net profit."

Subsequent to performing some quick arithmetic, Mandalay divulged, "You know, I anticipate Secretariat going post-ward at odds of 9/5 and obviously, 10% of 1.8 million is $180,000! Gosh, maybe I'm stupid to say this Commander, but that's quite an exorbitant potential commission!"

141

"Mm, especially when you consider how elementary your assignment is." Ross added. "So then, do we have an accord?"

Following a carefree shrug, Mandalay reasoned, "Well, I'm not exactly sold on the notion that Secretariat is a shoe in. That said, hey, what have I got to lose?"

Instead of wasting his time with a rhetorical question, Sir Barton's adulterous owner persisted with, "Then we'll meet beside Equine Chateau #1 at midnight on the eve of the race. Thereupon, you'll receive the aforementioned monies."

Of a mind that he could now digress, Jerome Park's "marionette" for that reason came out with, "You know I must say, it's kind of atypical isn't it Commander? I mean to trust a perfect stranger with one million dollars."

Without a hint of hesitation, Ross justified, "I pride myself on being an excellent judge of character sir. Uh besides, Heaven is a big place, but it's not that big."

"Mm, I get the picture." Mandalay gulped. "Ah, well, I suppose then there's nothing left to say except, until we meet again!"

First blocking his accomplice's escape, Ross then added, "Yes, and in the interim mister, mum's the word!"

Showing off his newfangled shoes in the process, Sir Barton ultimately sauntered onto Jerome Park's racing surface at 11:45 AM. Standing at the gap so he could "sign-off" on Ethan Bishop's supposed miracle glue, the "King of Wall Street" kept right on swirling his olive laden Bloody Mary as H.G. Bedwell briefed, "Give me a lap at half speed Johnny."

In that he was facing a do or die situation, Bedwell could barely look on as Sir Barton's burly frame bounded away. Soon reunited with a racer who was (at last) "firing on all cylinders", the gap's "nervous Nellie" next received that gift which mattered most (i.e., Leonard Jerome's nod of approval).

The product of being handed a whole new lease on life, Bedwell literally pounced on his groom ahead of pronouncing, "Well don't just stand there Toots! Go rustle us up an exercise rider so we can breeze him!"

Chapter 12 - A Crooked Road Made Straight

On account of stopping to swap out a flat tire for a stranded mother of three, Billy Turner wound up pulling into Jerome Park thirty minutes behind schedule. Ultimately scurrying the entire length of shed row, Seattle Slew's tardy trainer reached Equine Chateau #10 just in time to see Jean Cruget ravenously bite into an oversized bacon egg and cheese bagel. Short on wind yet still a slave to his sarcastic nature, Turner therefore "took a knee" before he drolly gasped, "You do know that the weight assignment for this race is 126 pounds right?"

Rather than wait until after he had swallowed, Cruget casually garbled, "The breakfast sandwiches they make over at Bathsheba's Bistro are out of this world Billy. You should try one sometime."

Once he was back on his feet, Turner piled on, "You should try showing some mercy pal. I pity Slew's spine."

"Will you stop." the backside's gorger groaned. "I mean seriously Billy; in all our years together, did I ever once walk into the paddock even one ounce over my riding weight? Take my word man, come December 31st, that scale up in the Jockeys' Room will read exactly 113 lbs.!"

"My ulcer will be the size of a Morgan silver dollar by then." Turner moaned. "Ugh, just hurry up and finish that Dagwood will ya! We've got work to do."

Consequent to collecting a compliant head nod, Mickey and Karen Taylor's antsy conditioner expeditiously entered Equine Chateau #10. Having rolled out of bed with a specific strategy in mind, Turner nevertheless patiently heeded his horseman's sixth sense as it whispered, *"Exercise* him in-between two workhorses so he remembers what it's like to get bumped around a little." Following a successful retaliation by Mr. Left Brain that sounded like, "Nonsense, there'd be too much of a chance that he would get injured," Turner turned around and yelled, "Quit snacking and give me a hand Jean! I want to breeze before the strip gets too congested!"

Upon making his grand entrance, Cruget blabbed, "Know something funny boss? Mr. Barrera said the exact same thing to Cauthen's sub just before you got here."

Now because he'd been firmly focused on his faction's affairs, Billy Turner hadn't given any thought to the fact that his Champion's roommate was absent. (Though initially received as a short-term tenant, Louis Wolfson's entry became a lasting fixture after Mickey Taylor left a voicemail which conveyed, "Good morning Mr. Jerome. Uh, Karen and I have talked it over and instead of you scrambling to rebuild Equine Chateau #11, we think it best that Affirmed just remain our guest.")

Soon given a leg up on the fringe of Equine Chateau #10's foraging field, Jean Cruget thereupon made headway towards Heaven's only operable racing oval. Promptly snowed under by a chorus of construction, Seattle Slew's chagrined conductor thus complained, "Bleachers huh? It sounds more like they're building London Bridge!"

"Dealing with this exceptional noise level will be excellent practice for him!" Turner ventilated. "Rest assured, the combined clamor of five hundred thousand fans is going to parallel a nuclear explosion!"

145

Since this was his first visit to the Main Grandstand's upper level, Laz Barrera took a quick look around before he parked it next to Steve Cauthen. In back of beholding the primary symptom of prolonged insomnia, Affirmed's hot-tempered trainer tongue-lashed, "Man for the tenth time, go and pick up some Jujupe Nighttime Tea from "Philemon's Pharmacy" over on 79th street. Then you won't have to stagger around like a zombie."

Through the tail end of yet another lengthy yawn, "The Kid" responded, "His breeze Laz, his breeze. That's what I want to talk about."

While he watched Seattle Slew swiftly step off from the five-eighths pole, Barrera straightforwardly summarized, "We need a little more early foot if we're gonna secure our usual mid-stalking position. Mm, I could slap some blinkers on. You know, try to squeeze a bit more speed out of him that way."

Instead of commenting on the proposed equipment change, "The Kid" went and remarked, "You know nothing against *Juan Carlos* boss, but our guy tends to break flat if he's not especially fond of who's calling the shots. Ugh, what I wouldn't do to be back at the helm!"

As a now "cooled down" Affirmed was walked off the track courtesy of his temporary exercise rider, Barrera consoled, "I know you're frustrated Steve but seeing as how this is Mr. Jerome's joint, we're therefore bound by Doctor Luke's orders. I mean, where he is coming from makes sense though. For safety's sake, you really shouldn't ride until your arm is fully operational."

"Doc says I won't be near one hundred percent 'till around Christmas!" Cauthen huffed. "Great. So, if we're talking best case scenario, I'm up for what, his final breeze? Man, I can't recoup my timing inside of one session!"

After he'd thrown an arm around his pessimistic pal, Barrera laughed, "Oh please, give me a break! Why you'll forget how to ride Affirmed on the same day that I forget how to make Café con Leche!"

Because he wanted to avoid a certain sect of early risers who'd been berating his riotous racer, Ben Jones had secretly scheduled a late afternoon training session. Presently standing directly aside Equine Chateau #5's turbo-jet rectangular hot tub, Calumet's senior conditioner first made a slight adjustment to Whirlaway's custom "right side only" blinkered hood before he outlined, "Hey Al, when we get out there I want you to walk him twice around directly aside the inner rail. Err, I know this discipline hasn't kept him from bolting thus far, however something is telling me not to give up."

Following the thirty minutes it took to complete his introductory assignment, Snider settled alongside the gap to the tune of, "Good. Next is a nice controlled warm up lap to see if you guys can actually get along."

Behind giving an "O.K." sign, Eddie Arcaro's eager replacement reached for the whip that was tucked in the back pocket of his blue jeans. Having been down this road before, Ben Jones as a result cautioned, "Uh, just so you know Al, he won't tolerate the stick unless he's in an actual race."

"I'm just taking this along as a precaution." Snider pledged. "You know, so I can administer a love tap should he start to swerve."

In the course of thinking, *"Fine, learn the hard way,"* Ben Jones formally cleared Calumet's "four-legged conundrum" for takeoff. Now although he began wandering to and fro right from the get-go, Whirlaway was in no way content with executing just his average shenanigans. So it was that as he entered the far turn, the horse known as "Mr. Longtail" threw a fit that would have made a rodeo bull jealous.

Along with feeling what it was like to be a toddler's ragdoll, Jerome Park's unnerved pilot similarly saw that he was about to be rudely "introduced" to Jerome Park's inelastic outer rail. Suddenly faced with the prospect of phoning 911 to request an ambulance, Ben Jones for this reason unhesitatingly cried, "Pull back on him boy! Pull back I say!"

Now because he'd gone and employed the tightest possible rein, Snider soon got Whirlaway moving in the right direction again. Still, because his heart couldn't handle any more close shaves, Jones subsequently charged, "Come back in boy! Come back in this instant!"

Whereas he was bound and determined to quell "Mr. Longtail's" bratty behavior, the strip's budding "bronco-buster" elected to turn a deaf ear. (Of course the instant he was "unshackled", Warren Wright Sr.'s wackadoodle went right back to causing chaos.) Once again on a direct collision course with the strip's peripheral barrier, Snider hence concluded that it was better to break his word rather than his neck.

In that same moment where he felt a rigid right handed whip, Whirlaway made an abrupt ninety degree left hand turn. Suddenly spewed from the saddle, Al Snider consequently performed a perfect mid-air pirouette (on his way towards a crash landing).

Even though he had every right to jump all over his insubordinate jockey, Ben Jones instead blew in like a worried mother hen. Flushed in the cheeks from having left most of his breath on Jerome Park's backstretch, the strip's second fastest being nevertheless calmly examined his rider's badly fractured index finger before he stressed, "You need Doctor Luke boy. First though, we gotta corral that crackpot."

While he motioned his head, Snider resentfully said, "Should be easy enough, he's standing right behind you."

In the process of spinning around, Ben Jones literally knocked noses with his long-tailed renegade. Never before mocked by the equine species, Heaven's most frustrated horseman responded by bewailing, "Besides a splint, Doc better also have some sedatives Al 'cause I'm telling you; this horse has got me on the verge of a nervous breakdown!"

On the heels of hearing Doctor Luke author a positive prognosis, Ben Jones spent a few hours isolated inside of Equine Chateau #5. Finally getting to a place where he could go and calmly tell his boss about the day's catastrophe, Calumet's senior conditioner thereupon dragged himself out the door and onto shed row. Soon absorbed with the golden glow of dusk, Jones therefore jumped back a bit when he heard, "How's Snider doing Ben? I heard he had a pretty nasty spill out there today."

As he shook James Fitzsimmons' weather beaten hand inside of the shadow that was being cast by Equine Chateau #3, Whirlaway's warden got across, "Well his right index finger looks like a purple pretzel, however Doctor Luke said he'll still be able to ride. That is, if he can actually manage to stay in the irons."

Since he especially esteemed the soul he was speaking with, "Sunny" Jim sincerely sympathized, "Well, there's no question that Whirlaway is a tough nut to crack Ben but believe you me, I can relate to what you're going through. I mean don't forget, I've got a wild one in my own barn as well."

After he'd set his attention on the humongous chestnut head that was now protruding through the upper portion of Equine Chateau #3's horizontally divided front door, Jones acknowledged, "Yeah, ain't that the truth. And speaking of, how is Omaha faring these days?"

"Mm, I've been fiddling around with his intake here recently." Fitzsimmons confessed. "Actually, that's the

150

reason why I'm here so late. Making sure, you know, that he cleans his dinner plate."

With the most unpresumptuous tone he could muster, Calumet's senior conditioner asked, "Granted it's none of my business, but why the change in diet?"

Transparent as they came, "Sunny" Jim resultantly turned towards the "Belair Bullet" and then revealed, "Well, I've been feeding my guys twenty-five percent alfalfa since it helps promote energy right. The problem is Omaha's been kicking down the walls at night! Therefore, the menu now consists of just oats and plain old pasture grass. Yes sir, that's the recipe to employ if they're running "a little hot"."

"Heavens to Betsy I must be blind!" Jones abruptly exclaimed. "Why, I've been supplementing Whirlaway's supper with alfalfa for the past eleven weeks!"

Positive that the root cause of "Mr. Longtail's" bothersome behavior had finally been unearthed, Fitzsimmons accordingly aired, "Oh dear, no wonder why he's been so short-fused! C'mon then Ben, I have a hundred pound bag of whole-food oats and a few extra bails of pasture grass out in my pickup truck. Yes sir, why we'll fix that rambunctious racer of yours from the inside out!"

Chapter 13 - Making Up for Lost Time

With the aid of two arms that were pumping like a pair of auto pistons, Warren Mehrtens again dashed from the eighth-pole towards Jerome Park's finish line. Now though not a huge fan of executing intermittent wind sprints, Assualt's exceptionally athletic jockey was nonetheless, an absolute stickler when it came to staying in shape. (Asked throughout his career why he worked out harder than ninety-nine percent of those who shared his profession, Mehrtens had always answered with, "Losing I can handle. Losing because another rider outworked me is something that I can't handle.")

Concurrent to crossing the wire, the oval's lone inhabitant heard his "smart watch" start to chime. Using the inner rail as a crutch as he gasped "Hello", Mehrtens next took in a short pause and then the melody of, "Well, I had to soften him up with a few shots of barrel proof bourbon; however he finally gave me the green light to reinstate you."

Once he'd suppressed his elation, Assault's regular pilot probed, "Here's what I don't get though Max, why was Kleberg so hesitant? I mean, obviously my Sciatica is no longer an issue. Otherwise, I wouldn't be out here impersonating a roadrunner!"

"His hesitation didn't have anything to do with your Sciatica." Hirsch forthrightly assured. "Look, between us, he's scared that you're gonna take another spill and miss the race. See man, the boss always praises Pastel, yet deep down, he knows who Assault really responds to. Anyway hey, I'm walking into the feed store so let me let you go. I'll

152

see you tomorrow morning at the barn say, a little after seven."

Per his instructions, Warren Mehrtens infiltrated the black walnut paneled interior of Equine Chateau #7 at 7:07 AM the next morning. Already sitting beside Homely the mutt at a small corner table, Robert J. Kleberg and Pastel Garcia quietly sipped their coffee as Max Hirsch stepped away from Assault and outlined, "Zero hour if fast approaching Warren so it's time to ratchet it up a notch. I mean ideally, I'd like to see three-quarters today in 1:11 flat."

While he admiringly looked upon the "Club Footed Comet's" defining characteristic, Mehrtens confidently told, "Just lead me to the gap sir."

Despite being razor sharp at the start of his warm up, Assault came counterclockwise around the clubhouse turn looking like a complete kindergartener. Convinced his racer's revolt had been spawned by the fierce construction that was taking place alongside Leonard Jerome's mansion, Max Hirsch accordingly commanded, "Go fetch me a set of full cup blinkers Pastel. If we blind him to this bedlam, perhaps he'll be less agitated."

Although away from the gap for less than five minutes, Garcia ultimately reassembled with not only his own crew, but also the recently arrived squadron of: H.G. Bedwell, Johnny Loftus, Toots Thompson, Ethan Bishop and Sir Barton. Well aware that Assault was worth ten times more than the workhorse that was being loosened up out on the oval, Bedwell therefore ended his extemporaneous sales pitch with, "You have to admit that it makes sense Max. Look, we're both looking to add a lot more endurance right? Man I'm telling you, if we put our boys through a rough and tumble match race, why their fitness levels will go through the roof!"

Whereas he was skeptical about the substance that held Sir Barton together, the "Club Footed Comet's" conditioner warily responded, "I know Harvey, but it's just that I have some apprehension concerning those glued on shoes. I mean if we're sitting second and one flies off; I may have to break out the smelling salts!"

Compelled to intercede, Ethan Bishop thus stepped forward and then specifically explained, "Fear not Mr. Hirsch. The Caulobacter Crescentus bacterial cement I've been employing grips 10,000 pounds per square inch! In fact, you're looking at a seal that can only be rendered void through the use of industrial-strength Hydrogen Fluoride!"

Thanks in large part to Bishop's elaborate scientific testimonial, Hirsch eventually warmed up to the idea of a six furlong match race. Forced to think on the fly after a succeeding coin toss awarded Assault the strip's inside lane, H.G. Bedwell thereupon turned to Johnny Loftus and whispered, "We're faster from the blocks so floor it for the first forty yards and then angle in. We'll swipe the rail from right underneath their noses."

For the reason that his eyes had stayed fixed on Sir Barton, Warren Merhtens dropped his riding gloves as he was being given a leg up. Once he'd dusted off and handed back these crucial articles, Hirsch benignly admonished, "There's no reason to over think this son. And don't worry if you lose sight of him early, he'll come back to you in the stretch."

In back of limbering up their Champions on opposite ends of the strip, Johnny Loftus and Warren Mehrtens made dock at the three-quarters pole. Positioned out in the "two path", Sir Barton now started jostling around like a Mexican jumping bean however because he'd been outfitted with full cup blinkers, Assault missed most of the show. (Obliged all the same to don his "psychologist hat", Merhtens consequently breathed, "That's it, pay him no mind boy. He's just trying to get in your head.")

(One byproduct of the pending preliminary bout was that Jerome Park's apron had become a breeding ground for "action" both big and small. Dragged into the fray after being approached by the owner of Sal's Mid-Town Italian Café, Pomeroy J. Mandalay in fact now had five thousand good reasons to root for the contestant with the clubbed hoof.)

In that he was getting sick of holding down a half-ton of hyper horseflesh, Johnny Loftus impatiently yapped, "Just say when partner!"

Though he tried to "get the drop" on his foe with a premature shout of, "Okay go!" Warren Mehrtens only wound up discombobulating his downstairs' neighbor. None too thrilled about Assualt's flat-footed break (and face that was now covered in "kickback"), Robert J. Kleberg hence scornfully thought, *"Ugh, way to go Warren."*

Despite owning the velocity of a plummeting roller coaster car, the strip's "leading man" wasn't free to just sit back and enjoy the ride. Presently driving down the "center lane" because Sir Barton had taken off at an askew angle, Johnny Loftus actually ended up eyeballing his left rein just prior to H.G. Bedwell's adamant shout of, "What in the world are you doing way out there?!"

Subsequent to snagging his trainer's attention, Robert J. Kleberg started to openly criticize the man who'd put his horse behind the 8-ball. Yet again breaking his earlier vow "not to play referee", a more than adamant Max Hirsch promptly kept the peace by promising, "It's going to be fine sir. Trust me."

Back some ten lengths as he entered the far turn, Warren Mehrtens therefore wasn't exactly what'd you'd call optimistic. However, inside of that moment where he recalled the words, "...he'll come back to you in the stretch," the strip's straggling pilot came to realize what Max Hirsch (and Pomeroy J. Mandalay) had known all along. (Namely, that the strip's current leader was still well behind the curve in terms of competitive stamina.)

Formerly stationed just behind the inner rail at the head of the straightaway, a Wood Stork's sudden flight prompted Sir Barton to bolt back out into the center of the racetrack. As bad as this freak incident was though, Johnny Loftus had an even bigger problem in that his tiring mount simply refused to "change leads". *(American racehorses typically travel turns on their left lead and straight avenues on their right lead. Now if a racer doesn't switch leads in a timely fashion, they will fatigue exponentially. This is analogous to someone switching a heavy bag from their left hand to their right hand as they stroll through a shopping mall.)*

Since he owned a nose that could "smell blood in the water", Assault quickened on his own when he saw that he'd received a double portion of favor. Savvy this was no time to micromanage, Warren Mehrtens for that reason bottled up his whip as he told, "O.K. boy, you're calling the shots now!"

With seventy yards left to go, Johnny Loftus completely gave up on the possibility of being saved by the wire. Ultimately resorting to the oldest trick in the book, Sir Barton's frantic jockey now intentionally drifted in a lane however this "peripheral intimidation tactic" was easily thwarted by those same full cup blinkers which had "intervened" back at the three-quarters pole. In the mood to rub it in a little as he came through on the rail, Pomeroy J. Mandalay's new favorite rider as a result razzed, "That chintzy stunt doesn't work when they can't see you sliding over Johnny!"

In the wake of scoring by just over two and a half lengths, Warren Mehrtens embarked on a leisurely victory lap. Waiting with open arms back at the gap, Max Hirsch showed off the face of his digital stopwatch and then smirked, "Well looky there, you nailed it boy! Yep, three-quarters in 1:11 flat!"

Upon hanging his head, Assault's dust coated jock indignantly said, "Huh, too bad I flubbed the start, otherwise he gets home in 1:09."

An admitted sore loser, Johnny Loftus thus avoided the gap area until Kleberg and company were gone from sight. Someone who distained defeat ten times more than Jerome Park's vanquished jockey, H.G. Bedwell nevertheless led his team in to the tune of, "Well let's look at the bright spots: his shoes are staying on, he's training without a lick of pain and man, he looked like an African gazelle going down the backstretch."

"I think deep down we all knew that he needed a tightener." Loftus arbitrarily added. "Yeah, it's like my grandpa used to say, 'Sometimes you have to sacrifice a battle in order to win the war.'"

Chapter 14 - A Golden Invitation

As he slowly descended down into the center of Equine Chateau #4's Chesterfield lounge seat, Samuel D. Riddle sharply called his organization's weekly administrative meeting to order. Opening his mouth at exactly 7:00 AM, George Conway thereupon detailed, "Tactically speaking, I'd say we're in a rather enviable position sir. I mean, both Loftus and Longden know that their speedsters aren't in good enough shape to press us early and then remain competitive. On that account, I predict that Charlie here will fall heir to an uncontested lead and if that indeed ends up being the case, well then you'd better have the champagne on standby!"

"Don't reserve our spot in the Winner's Enclosure just yet!" Riddle scolded. "Less we forget, Christmas is but four days away and War Admiral still refuses to school! Ha, you dare sit there and talk about my horse going wire to wire? Uh, what you need to be telling me is how you plan on getting his rear end into the starting gate!"

In back of being shot down like a clay pigeon, Conway contended, "Like I told you over dinner last week sir, smashing through the doors of stall #1 like that messed him up a little psychologically. However if yesterday's near go is any indication, then we should see our desired result here within the hour."

While nodding his head to show that he agreed, Charlie Kurtsinger noticed something gliding across the floor. Wrapped in platinum bullion foil, the oversized envelope that had been slid beneath War Admiral's front door ultimately traveled a good twenty feet before it clipped the tip of a certain brown Oxford dress shoe. Subsequent to breaking Leonard Jerome's personal wax seal, Samuel Riddle liberated a seven square inch 14kt gold billet which read,

~To those Connections associated with War Admiral

Your presence is requested at...

A Transcendental Gala Dinner
To be held inside of Jerome Park's
Illustrious Clubhouse
On December 30th at 6:00 PM
Black Tie Required
Please RSVP no later than December 27th

Sincerely, Leonard Jerome & August Belmont~

Made to "turn cartwheels" by their unexpected bounty, George Conway and Charlie Kurtsinger in fact carried on like two teenagers until Samuel D. Riddle sternly bid, "Uh, do you mind gentlemen?! We have a schedule to keep!"

After he'd authored a prolonged apology, Conway guaranteed, "We'll be out of here in less than five minutes sir!"

Understandably concerned because his horse had been deliberately kicking the chute's gilded apparatus,

Riddle accordingly pointed at a gory scab ahead of conclusively ordering, "I want those legs wrapped and I mean good before we head out George. He's accumulated enough scar tissue for one season!"

Instead of the same spacious gap they'd come to know and love, Samuel D. Riddle's squadron wound up walking up to a five meter inlet that was wedged between two sections of temporary bleachers. Totally taken aback by August Belmont's architectural brain child, George Conway hence did a "double take" before he declared, "Can you believe that they finished this monstrosity of a project ten days ahead of schedule?!"

Since admiring Jerome Park's latest add-on was way down on his list of priorities, War Admiral's antsy owner went and pressed, "If you please Mr. Conway, I want to be on time for my brunch engagement with *Commodore Vanderbilt*!"

Soon stepping into the presence of a miracle that was twice the size of Belmont's bleachers, Conway consequently gasped, "Well will you look at that!"

(Whizzing down the homestretch straight as an arrow, Whirlaway was currently dazzling those same railbirds who had left him for dead. First taking a quick "praise break" over inside the paddock, Ben Jones next "scrolled down" to "Sunny" Jim's phone number so he could text, **"Your dietary recommendations did the trick! I'm**

indebted to you brother. And BTW, if I were you, I wouldn't tell Woodward about how you aided Calumet's cause. ☺")

As Jerome Park's equine masseur continued to work the knots out of Omaha's lower back, Willie "Smokey" Saunders lent his attention to an adjacent tear-away wall calendar which read, "**SATURDAY - DEC. 24ᵗʰ**". Now just one hour prior, Equine Chateau #3's 109 lb. bystander had found himself on the cusp of a rare solo breeze yet at the very last moment, James Fitzsimmons had flip-flopped, "You know on second thought, just go for a two mile gallop Willie. I want him fresh for Monday's final bout."

Soon parked on shed row enjoying his second favorite pastime, Saunders continued to "puff away" up until the personage of one August Belmont appeared. Gallant as well as dashing, Leonard Jerome's hallowed lieutenant therefore tipped his Edwardian style silk plush top hat prior to telling, "Sir I must say, that bruiser of yours looked smashingly good during his gallop today!"

With his cigar still stuck in his mouth, Omaha's conductor recounted, "Full of himself he was sir, and when you see them dappled all over like that, it means they're ready to run a big one!"

"Well this is when you want to see them peaking." Belmont promulgated. "At any rate my boy, I need a word with Mr. Woodward. Have you any idea of his present whereabouts?"

Once he'd removed the article that had been inhibiting his speech, Saunders clearly surmised, "I want to say that he's watching Mr. Fitzsimmons gate-school Gallant Fox. Nothing's wrong is there sir?"

Through a composed chuckle, Belmont divulged, "No my boy. I just wanted to tell him that the post position draw ceremony and press conference for our little year-end pageant will take place inside of the Clubhouse on Wednesday between the hours of 4:00 PM and 7:00 PM. You know and incidentally, almost every media representative who is scheduled to attend has expressed an interest in speaking with your horse's trainer."

While wincing, Saunders energetically asserted, "Good luck with that! The old man hates being interviewed!"

"Mm, so I have heard." Belmont moaned. "Nevertheless, for the sake of public relations, we all must cooperate and eh "play the game" as they say. You know frankly, Mr. Jerome doesn't exactly fancy the microphone either! Although, since he plans on releasing the much anticipated morning line after the draw, an intense Q&A session seems inevitable."

"Personally, pari-mutuals have never interested me." Saunders shrugged. "Still and all, if I were a horseplayer's piggy bank, I'd be a little worried right now!"

Without missing a beat, the backside's best dressed soul added, "Petrified is more like it! Ha, and believe me my boy, it is about to be open season on safety deposit boxes too! See, as a race day courtesy, this property is going to operate a provisional bullion exchange where punters will be able to liquidate their pure precious metals and certified diamonds."

After his astonishment had worn off, shed row's smoke loving saint acknowledged, "Those with guts enough to bet gold and gems have my utmost respect governor. Yet if given the choice, I would trade the deed to Fort Knox for a trip to Jerome Park's Winner's Enclosure."

Because he had been blessed with abounding discernment, Belmont bore a confident smile as he revealed, "Rest assured son; that much I already knew."

In the midst of turning a little red, Saunders digressed, "Uh, well then, shall I tell Mr. Woodward that you stopped by sir?"

"I'd be indebted if you would." Belmont replied. "Oh, and in the course of enjoying tomorrow's festivities, please remember to thank our Lord for His grace. Without it, there'd be no race, or anything else worth celebrating for that matter."

As he stuck his stogie back between his teeth, Saunders shouted, "Amen to that!! And on behalf of Belair, a very Merry Christmas to you sir!!"

Chapter 15 - Completing the Work Tab

Since the *Savior's* birthday party was every saint's top priority, Heaven's only operating racetrack remained totally dark throughout Christmas Day. First light on Monday, December 26th however marked the beginning of Jerome Park's biggest event to date (particularly, a two-day affair that Pomeroy J. Mandalay had informally dubbed, "*The Festival of Final Workouts*").

Fully comprehending the occasion's gravity yet admittedly still half asleep, Jean Cruget thus tiredly yawned, "You still looking for just a maintenance breeze boss?"

As he watched his team breach the gap, Billy Turner coached, "That's what the manual calls for when they're dead fit Jean. So accordingly, I'll take five-eighths in say, 'round sixty two or sixty three. And remember, an injury this late in the game means we miss the dance so don't compromise your concentration out there today!"

In the wake of a guarded ten minute warm-up which wrapped up at 6:18 AM, Cruget blasted off in front of just over seventy-five thousand turf enthusiasts. Now as his ballpoint pen began to record, "*S. Slew - 5F fst 1:02 2/5 B - All systems are go,*" Pomeroy J. Mandalay abruptly heard a neighbor ostentatiously advertise, "Rumor has it that Wright's big gun is on deck folks!"

In back of punching in at a quarter 'till seven, Citation effortlessly strung together six furlongs in an absolutely "sick" 1:09 4/5. This just for starters, "Big Cy" then capped his near perfect training season by galloping out an additional mile in 1:36 4/5! Coincidentally catching glimpse of Adelphia Armour during the cool down process, Eddie Arcaro thereupon thought, *"It's time to hit the panic button sweetheart."*

"Placed in the ring" as Citation left the building, William Woodward Sr.'s dynamic duo utterly refused to acknowledge one another as they warmed up for what would be their final head to head confrontation. A soul who secretly wanted to see Omaha "get off the schnide", James Fitzsimmons as a result ultimately governed, "Today's bout will be over five furlongs of ground men! Line up on the rail Saunders, and I want you to call the start!"

Following an even break, "Sunny" Jim's students seesawed back and forth through a hot opening quarter mile that was clocked in :21 3/5. Eventually eyelevel with a riding boot that was monogrammed "*WS*", a desperate Gallant Fox therefore decided to "cross the dividing line" midway around the far turn. Suddenly in tight against the wood, Saunders recouped his balance and then rightly fussed, "C'mon Earl, give me some breathing room will ya!"

As he continued to futilely wrestle his "Rock of Gibraltar", Sande legitimately defended, "There's nothing I can do when he gets like this Willie! Hopefully he'll let go of you in the lane!"

Now despite a tremendous temptation to counter attack with seventeen hands worth of exasperated equine brawn, Jerome Park's hindered jockey wasn't interested in seeing an evening headline which read, "**Saunders Intentionally Bowls Over Stable Mate During Final Breeze!!!**"

On the other side of missing by just a nose (this despite being completely manhandled most of the way), Omaha dragged his despondent driver back towards the gap. Silent until the ranks were completely restored, James Fitzsimmons then aired, "They came home in :59 2/5 gentlemen, all in all not bad. What was your impression of them?

Rather than ignore the "elephant in the room", Earl Sande immediately acknowledged, "My guy initiated a lot of contact sir, we're probably looking at a different result otherwise."

After a long drawn out sigh, "Sunny" Jim poked, "How 'bout it Willie? Did you get knocked around out there?"

Deciding to take the high road for his friend's sake, the day's second-place pilot hence whitewashed, "No excuses sir. The best horse won."

Since it was clear by now that Saunders simply wanted to "get on with his day", Fitzsimmons promptly deviated, "Alright boys, let's head in. From here on out it's just a matter of keeping them happy."

     Wrapping up his pre-race preparations with an easy one mile jog, Count Fleet was consequently on scene for all of five minutes. Stowing his stopwatch for the time being, Pomeroy J. Mandalay then kept busy by way of journalizing, *"Seeing as how Count Fleet doesn't really own an official breeze, it will be most interesting to see what kind of morning line Mr. Jerome attaches."*

     A horse who was definitely "all the rage" (thanks to his recent match race result), Assault actually acted up a little before he confidently commenced his 8:30 AM "dress rehearsal". Now because Max Hirsch had ordered an ascending six furlong drill, the "Club Footed Comet's" final clocking of 1:12 3/5 was much more impressive than it looked on paper. In fact, Pomeroy J. Mandalay's right hand literally shook from excitement as it documented, *"...covered last quarter in 21 seconds flat!"*

Day Two

Subsequent to setting down his binoculars, George Conway picked up his tablet and typed, "**Dec. 27ᵗʰ - off @ approx. 7:08 AM ~ 7f fst 1:21 4/5 B**". Eventually walking back up to Section 2B, War Admiral's anxious conditioner then retook his seat before he softly apologized, "I know he went faster than you would have liked sir, however he stayed well within himself the entire time."

While he indignantly pointed his brass handled quartz cane, Samuel D. Riddle snapped, "Uh, it's what occurred before, not during the workout that concerns me Mr. Conway! Now here's a news flash, we can't win if he doesn't load in! So if you don't mind, get your backside down those stairs and figure out a way to stick my horse into that blasted starting gate!"

Hardly the sentimental type, Laz Barrera nevertheless got a lump in his throat as he gave Steve Cauthen a leg up behind the gap. Suddenly hearing a few isolated "hoots and hollers", Affirmed's concerned conditioner therefore felt compelled to remind, "Again, stay in control of your emotions son 'cause like I said earlier, every railbird in this place is gonna go nuts when they realize you're back in the saddle."

Undoubtedly bolstered by the sound of his name being chanted, "The Kid" resultantly masterminded a six furlong maneuver that mirrored "Big Cy's" latest masterpiece! Made to grin like "a cat that had caught a canary", Barrera then "high-fived" his incoming jockey as he cried, "That's what I'm talking about! And you were so worried about your timing being off!"

Even though there was nothing wrong with a seven furlong time of 1:23 1/5, Sir Barton's satisfactory swansong was partly overshadowed by a rather remiss gallop out. Opting to adopt a "glass half full" mentality, Johnny Loftus thus returned to the gap exclaiming, "He's come a mighty long way in just four weeks sir!"

In back of listening to Jerome Park's turquoise clock tower toll for the ninth and final time, H.G. Bedwell bemoaned, "I'd give my right arm for ten additional days with him Johnny. A few more breezes that's all. Just so he could build up one last nugget of stamina. As it stands, you'll reach the bottom of him at the eighth-pole."

"Man not that same old speech again!" Loftus clamored. "I mean, you said the exact same thing five minutes before we went out to warm up for the Kentucky Derby!"

An outgrowth of getting the antithesis of what he'd asked for, Lucien Laurin pressed his skull against the paddock's 14kt gold perimeter gate ahead of griping, "So much for an easy half mile! Get a load of this Mrs. Chenery!"

As she took hold of a stopwatch that read :44 3/5, Secretariat's cultivated owner called up, "Like you always say..."

"Ain't it the truth?!" Laurin interrupted. "And I'll say it again ma'am! "Big Red" goes wherever and does whatever he wants!"

Creatively called a, *"Five furlong brunch time breeze,"* Whirlaway's crowning practice run had also inspired Pomeroy J. Mandalay to pen, *"Not quite a "worst to first" turnaround here, but close."*

Now though there was no way of knowing what the stopwatch read, Al Snider could tell from Ben Jones' theatrics that "Mr. Longtail" had hit an upper deck home run. Currently galloping out past the Main Grandstand yet still able to hear his chieftain celebrate, Snider snickered and then justifiably thought, *"This from the same guy who insisted he be scratched."*

Chapter 16 - The Post Position Draw

Numbering nine if counted, those circular "Connections' Tables" that sat inside of Leonard Jerome's spacious downstairs parlor were all crowned with absolutely dazzling "team placards". (For example, Table #1's rectangular 14kt gold free standing signboard read, *"Commander J.K.L. Ross & Company"*.) Handcrafted especially for eternity's first ever post position draw by "Samuel's Signs and Designs", each team placard similarly shared its table space with: brand new bone china, sterling silver utensils, balloon crystal goblets and mulberry silk napkins.

Now because the post position draw for Heaven's Premier Horse Race was the biggest news story going, the "King of Wall Street's" downstairs parlor had been fringed with a total of 149 black leather club chairs. A soul who delighted in treating his houseguests like royalty, Leonard Jerome had therefore gone and magnified his mansion's perimeter "media thrones" with (get this) frontal fully loaded mother-of-pearl office consoles! (Since the press would likewise partake of the gourmet buffet that had been prepared by the Clubhouse's renowned culinary faction, an appropriate amount of polished mahogany lap trays were also "in the house".)

After he'd wholly inspected that area where turf history would be made, August Belmont meticulously fired up a Montecristo No. 2 torpedo cigar. Subsequently giving in to his curiosity, Leonard Jerome's top confidant next peered out at the credentialed mob that was camped on the

Clubhouse's capacious front porch. (Incidentally, in what was a preventative measure against a possible mob scene, the "King of Wall Street" had wisely arranged for the Connections to enter his abode via a rear egress.)

In that moment where he felt an unexpected tap on the shoulder, Jerome Park's "Vice President" simultaneously heard, "Eleven hours August! That is how long it took me to manufacture the morning line! Good golly, I must've dissected every spec of data twenty times over! I'm talking: lifetime past performances, workout tabs, pedigree profiles, trainer and jockey winning percentages, dosage indexes, you name it!"

Following a quick swivel turn, Belmont contended, "Granted, the layoff these equines are returning from begets a gray area my friend. Yet, you've always had the uncanny knack of knowing almost exactly how much money a racer will take at the windows. That being said, what do you presume the closing odds for Heaven's Premier Horse Race will be?"

"I can't let the cat out of the bag quite yet." Jerome insisted. "Understandably, there still might be a last second adjustment. It just depends on how the entries draw in."

Since the "art of waiting" was one of his specialties, Belmont casually came back with, "Fair enough sir. Now come, you must take a gander at this herd of newshounds!"

In back of being formally received by Horace at precisely 4:00 PM, the Connections were led into the Clubhouse's downstairs parlor by way of a secret service corridor. Staying "buttoned-up" behind a front of house brass lectern until everyone had found their seats, August Belmont thereafter publicized, "Esteemed Connections, I would like to formally welcome you to Jerome Park's Clubhouse and the highly anticipated post position draw for Heaven's Premier Horse Race! Now please be advised that once beverage orders are secured, our concierges will open the bilateral buffet line!"

At last ushered into the "King of Wall Street's" personal utopia at 4:15 PM, those with press credentials were next encouraged to grab their lap trays and "chow down". Someone who already desired "seconds", William Woodward Sr. accordingly found his way back to the resident carver as he advertised, "Hey you press-people I promise you this, if that prime rib doesn't absolutely knock your socks off, then I'll scratch both my racers!"

Ultimately reconnecting with his brass lectern at the hour of 5:00 PM, August Belmont then spiritedly imparted, "Esteemed Connections, respected members of the media, if I may have your attention. Please join me now in welcoming the primary sponsor of Heaven's Premier Horse Race and your master of ceremonies, Mr. Leonard Walter Jerome!"

As he took part in an ovation for the ages, Belmont also retreated towards the ruffled red velvet curtain that was directly behind him. Over fifty feet long and seventeen feet tall, this illuminated wall mounted drapery was soon drawn back with the intention of revealing a life-size magnetized 3D mural of Jerome Park's eleven-stall 14kt gold starting gate! (Concurrently brought out by two white-gloved valets, a self supported clear plastic globe which contained eleven "image-bearing" fiberglass spheres likewise generated widespread speculation.)

Following a grateful wave that helped deposit everyone back into their seats, Leonard Jerome specified, "Ladies and gentlemen, the post position selection order for Heaven's Premier Horse Race will be determined through the use of this unique battery powered clear plastic globe. Now when I activate this apparatus's built-in fan, the eleven image-bearing fiberglass spheres contained therein will first scatter around for a few seconds before they randomly drain down into this clear vertical underlying support tube. The owner linked to the equine likeness that appears on the uppermost sphere will consequently approach our 3D mural with arms wide open so that they might receive a monstrous magnetic "titled portrait" of their horse. Once my valets have supplied said magnet, our front and center owner will then be "on the clock". Meaning, they will have sixty seconds to select a post position by way of adhering their Champion's portrait to whichever "stall" they are smitten with. The second highest image bearing sphere will dictate which owner is "on deck" and so on and so forth. Err, now before we begin, I think it is right that I ask; does any owner object to the blueprint that has been put forth?"

When it was clear that ownership was "a-o.k." with everything, the "King of Wall Street" continued, "Then without further adieu, I will now set the image-bearing spheres in motion!"

(Already obsessing over her morning column, a reporter who'd been sent over from "The Happy Hunting Ground Herald" for that reason wrote, *"One could hear a pin drop inside of that moment where "Lady Luck" took control of the show."*)

Since it was his duty to relate each owner's fate, August Belmont donned his reading spectacles and then pronounced, "Kicking off the post position selection process will be none other than, Commander J.K.L. Ross!"

Having sat down with a pretty straightforward strategy, H.G Bedwell therefore immediately whispered, "Post #1 if you please sir."

In spite of the fact that he was soon clutching a monstrous magnetic "titled portrait" of Sir Barton, Ross' lone care actually pertained to what numeral Secretariat would ultimately wear. Pretending the entire time however that his Champion was top priority, Heaven's "luckiest" owner first "sewed up the rail" before he formally announced, "On the advice of my conditioner, Sir Barton will break from post position number one."

Someone who didn't take kindly to mutiny, H.G. Bedwell nevertheless kept a level head as he told his up in arms jockey, "I know you might get squeezed down in there but you have to remember that you're teamed with a horse that's only like seventy-five percent fit. I mean if we're going to have any chance at all, then we've got to save every possible inch of ground."

In the wake of August Belmont's second starchy sentence, Robert J. Kleberg hightailed it towards post #7. One who felt like it was Christmas all over again, Warren Mehrtens nonetheless stayed calm while he conveyed, "Thanks again for persuading him Max. Yeah, he can call me crazy all he wants, but that number has always been good to me."

Interlude - Receiving a Windfall

Now traditionally, post position is of greater consequence to those equines who prefer to race on or near the lead. Why you ask? Well, a speedster who is drawn outside must be "used early" in order to clear the field and cut over to the rail. Otherwise, they will get "hung wide" and "lose ground" going around the first turn. All the same, Ben Jones breathed an immense sigh of relief as he watched Warren Wright Sr. organize a rendezvous between Whirlaway and post #2. (In brief, because of his "adaptation walks" and "right side only" blinkered hood, "Mr. Longtail" had been settling into stride better when he was along towards the wood.)

Following Omaha's snappy pairing with post #3; Seattle Slew gained an unexpected date with post #8. Consequently landing four spots from the fence (all because Billy Turner had wanted to avoid the "Belair Bullet's" potentially hazardous bulk), Citation and Eddie Arcaro thus came away with a setup that held ample promise. See, since "Big Cy" possessed more early foot than both Omaha and Whirlaway, "The Master" could now see himself sliding over into a good initial ground saving position; one that (with a little luck) might even morph into a kind of "Catbird Seat". *(Catbird Seat - Refers to the highly advantageous "stalking" locale that is found directly behind two or more dueling pacesetters.)*

Conferred an absolute "no-brainer" (on account of Gallant Fox's implantation into post #5 and Secretariat's implantation into post #6), Louis Wolfson thereupon told his crew, "Post #9 huh? I guess it's simply Affirmed's destiny to remain alongside Seattle Slew."

Though dealt a fate that was far from great (i.e., post #10), Mrs. John D. Hertz's coddled front-runner wound up "hitting it big" compared to War Admiral. Someone who couldn't stand to see a grown man cry, George Conway resultantly reassured his owner, "Take it easy sir. I mean, we can still win from the eleven hole. This just means that Charlie has no margin for error."

Following a spell where everyone was allowed to catch their breath, Leonard Jerome rolled back his shoulders and stated, "Distinguished guests of the Clubhouse, the morning line for Heaven's Premier Horse Race is as follows: #1 - Sir Barton 25/1, #2 - Whirlaway 15/1, #3 - Omaha 12/1, #4 - Citation 2/1, #5 - Gallant Fox 8/1, #6 - Secretariat 9/5, #7 - Assault 10/1, #8 - Seattle Slew 5/1, #9 - Affirmed 10/1, #10 - Count Fleet 30/1, #11 - War Admiral 12/1."

Once the morning line was pasted on the downstairs parlor's "pseudo starting gate" (courtesy of a digital ceiling projector), August Belmont informed, "Ladies and gentlemen, before we open the floor to questions, I will present those precepts which will govern all things pari-mutual come Saturday."

In back of digging out the 3x5 index card that had been hiding in his back pocket, Belmont resolutely read, "Those inclined to wager on Heaven's Premier Horse Race may do so at any one of Jerome Park's five hundred pari-mutual teller stations between the hours of 10:00 AM and 5:59 PM. The following six "$2 minimum" wagers will be taken: win, place, show, exacta, trifecta and superfecta. At the request of Horse Racing Nation, a ten cent superfecta pool will also be instituted. Interested horseplayers may raise their stake by liquidating: .999 gold, .999 silver, .999 platinum and certified diamonds inside of Jerome Park's provisional bullion exchange. December 30th's closing market price will determine the dollar amount paid for all precious metals. In addition, monies swapped for certified diamonds will coincide with appraisals conducted by contracted Tiffany & Co. gemologists. Note: precious stone valuations are non-negotiable. Winning pari-mutual tickets may be converted to cash only, regardless of purchase method. Finally, Jerome Park's 9:00 PM closure marks the pari-mutual redemption deadline."

181

Pretty blasé for the first fifteen minutes, the post position draw's press conference finally got interesting when a pencil pusher from the Eternity Times put forth, "Please fill in the blank Mr. Jerome. The most challenging part of hosting Heaven's Premier Horse Race will be...?"

Now because he was still waiting on a substantial shipment of Charmin, the "King of Wall Street" unhesitatingly shot back, "Making sure that there is enough bathroom tissue in stock for five hundred thousand saints."

Already unmercifully split between: August Belmont, a cluttered desktop, and a day-timer page that was tabbed *"Dec. 29th"*, Leonard Jerome's attention was nevertheless yanked in yet a fourth direction when an assistant to the upstairs butler rolled in and revealed, "Forgive the intrusion sir, but *Mayor Mancini* is holding on line one."

After about five minutes of race related small talk, the "King of Wall Street" was calculatedly hit with, "By the way monsieur, did you read the editorial on Heaven's Premier Horse Race that ran in this morning's edition of the Eternity Times? I thought the writer made one especially interesting point. Namely, that if opened Saturday your infield could easily entertain upwards of 75,000 saints!"

As he leaned on the "recline button" that was on the left arm of his high-back executive desk chair, Jerome zealously defended, "I did read that editorial sir. What it didn't mention though was the fact that I I had my rolling infield re-sodded this past July. I mean call me selfish, however I'm not about to just sit back and watch as $275,000 worth of Zoysia grass gets trampled!"

"Mm, I can't blame you for that sir." Mayor Mancini murmured. "Well please know that I only mentioned the article in the first place because history shows that you were willing to let tens of thousands roost on your infield throughout Jerome Park's inaugural festival in 1866. Gosh, $275,000 huh? Yes, of course. I mean, that's not chicken feed."

Suddenly convicted by his conscious (because he spent way over $275,000 a year just pampering his personal stallions), the "King of Wall Street" hence u-turned, "Uh, tell you what Mayor, I'll go ahead and open up my infield on Saturday if your administration handles the ticketing. You see, the Clubhouse will be hosting a Transcendental Gala Dinner tomorrow evening and my "to do list" is ten pages long!"

With his next breath, Mayor Mancini rapturously related, "That sir is a deal! O.K. so, I will have my "I.T." guy set up an 8:00 AM "gratis admissions lottery" in connection with www.Heaven'sPremierHorseRace/Tickets.com. And to help get the word out, I will call over to the Eternity Times after we hang up. Shoot, why this news will probably take up the evening edition's entire front page!"

In back of saying "adieu", Jerome rolled his eyes and then tiredly admitted, "Despite the pleasures they've afforded, the last ninety-six days have done me in August."

Presently endowed with the power to provide a "shot in the arm", August Belmont for that reason walked over to the upstairs office's oblong Savannah mini-bar. Quick to hold up a Rogaska crystal decanter and some matching stemware, Belmont thereafter disclosed, "I originally intended to unveil this toddy tomorrow night Leonard however in light of your altruism, I think you deserve a treat. Behold, Oloroso Sherry! Sixty-eight years old!"

"Oloroso Sherry!" Jerome yelped. "My word, how did you ever acquire something so scarce?!"

While he attentively poured with both hands, Belmont expounded, "Well as you've probably heard, *King Solomon* recently opened up this incredibly ritzy tavern in that pocket-sized sector to the northeast of us. So, when his majesty contacted me last week to request a Luxury Box, I did a little horse trading. Ha, and believe you me Leonard, this libation is nothing compared to what you're gonna see at the Transcendental Gala Dinner!"

Successive to a sip toast aimed at his business partner's resourcefulness, Jerome sought the veranda for a breath of fresh air. Soon needing a drink more than ever, the "King of Wall Street" hence immediately downed the remaining portion of his hard beverage prior to delivering, "Come August, feast your eyes on this hodge-podge!"

Now though it'd taken many moons to do so, War Admiral had finally made his conditioner "cry uncle". However instead of giving up gracefully, George Conway bitterly barked, "I want this perverse animal ridden away from this starting gate and put out of my sight Charlie! Shoot, let Jerome's gate crew worry about him! And if they can't get him to load in, then we'll just have to scratch!"

Despite an acute temptation to smash his glass against the veranda's wrought iron railing, Leonard Jerome instead simply vented, "We're in a pickle here August, a real pickle! I mean; what are we going to do if the Admiral utterly refuses to complete the lineup come post time?!"

Rather than stand idly by while his best friend fell apart, Belmont kindly reminded, "Relax old boy! You said yourself that the gate crew you've assembled could temper a Tyrannosaurus Rex! Still, it might not be a bad idea to load War Admiral first. That way, if there is a delay, you won't have to leave the rest of the field all cooped up for forever and a day!"

"Pigs will fly before Riddle consents to that arrangement!" Jerome insisted. "Why I can hear him now, *'I'm sorry sir, but I can't be sure that War Admiral won't freak out and injure himself as he waits for the rest of the field to load in.'"*

Behind complementing his business partner on a spot-on impersonation, Belmont theorized, "The time to spring this on him is at the Gala. Yes sir, it's basic psychology 101; ahem, a soul under the influence of free food and drink is easily persuaded!"

Chapter 17 - The Transcendental Gala Dinner

Made up of ninety-nine moving parts, the symphony orchestra that was sitting on Leonard Jerome's front lawn was presently on the cusp of taking a cue from legendary conductor *Leonard Bernstein*. Ultimately emerging from their gilded palace as Claude Debussy's "Clair de Lune" began to play; Leonard Jerome and August Belmont subsequently stepped onto a preposterously wide and far-reaching Saxony style red shag carpet. Now even though both of Jerome Park's live-in aristocrats were absolutely "dressed to kill" (meaning they each had on: a hand tailored cashmere tuxedo, a beaver fur top hat, an ermine sash, a French cuffed Borrelli shirt with black pearl buttons and platinum horse head cufflinks), only the "King of Wall Street" had "coughed up" what was necessary to acquire a pair of midnight-black Aubercy diamond studded dress shoes.

Received as a Christmas gift from his business partner, August Belmont's platinum Presidential Rolex currently read 5:58 PM. In effect what you'd call "stunned" (because every item on the Gala's last second ten page "to do list" bore a red checkmark), the Clubhouse's second most bejeweled gentleman hence commented, "Well, somehow we pulled it all together Leonard, and with two whole minutes to spare!"

As he continued to swirl a snifter which contained four fluid ounces of Frapin Cuvée 1888 Cognac, Jerome ventilated, "Yes well don't get too comfortable sir. It would seem that our incipient callers are inbound!"

186

Interlude - A Most Lavish Libation

Hustling away faster than the horse drawn carriage that had intersected Jerome Park's gap, August Belmont thereafter ordered the Gala's Barman to pop open a bottle of 1907 Heidsieck "Shipwrecked" Champagne. Now though originally loaded onto a boat in 1916 that was bound for Russia (and his majesty Tsar Nicholas II); the aforementioned bubbly in fact never reached port (thanks to a German submarine). Finally salvaged after aging in Davy Jones' Locker for over eight decades, that alky which came to be known as "Shipwrecked Heidsieck" undoubtedly remains every sparkling wine connoisseur's "Holy Grail".

Though nothing could match the feeling of standing atop the Clubhouse's 14kt gold facial stairway, Leonard Jerome felt inclined to make one final inspection of the Courtyard's hors d'oeuvre tables. (This was actually an especially astute call since there was a sideboard that was ready to buckle beneath a dense deposit of: Wagyu beef filets, Chinese matsutake mushroom pies and honey glazed pheasant cutlets.) Soon angling the beluga caviar station a bit more towards the orchestra, the "King of Wall Street" next neatened up a "cheese stand" which featured: Gruyere

187

Swiss, Young Creamy Lancashire and Pecorino Foglie di Noce (i.e., a sheep's milk cheese that is traditionally wrapped in walnut leaves).

Seeing as how he had picked up the tab for everything, the "King of Wall Street" didn't feel all that guilty about walking away from the Courtyard's sushi bar with a mouthful of yellow fin tuna nigiri. (A tough choice considering that the Clubhouse's itamae had likewise pre-set dozens of: aori-squid, conger eel, abalone and octopus rolls.) Still in the process of enjoying his brandy, Leonard Jerome for that reason politely shook his head when the sushi bar's third assistant steward held up a tokkuri that was filled with Watari Bune Kame-no O Sake.

Interlude - An AM Epiphany

Per the help of a rectangular granite cooking counter and five hundred "cage-free" eggs, the Transcendental Gala's outdoor seafood chef would spend his evening stuffing "made-to-order omelets" with both lobster meat and Golden Osetra caviar. Of course since some folks had no taste for yolks, the Courtyard's "Deep Sea Delicatessen" was on stand-by with: Alaskan king crab legs, steamed mussels steeped in white wine sauce, blowfish brisket, raw Atlantic oysters, seared scallops wrapped in bacon, sea cucumbers, "fatback" clam chowder, giant grouper filets, swordfish steaks, coconut crab claws and jumbo shrimp cocktail. (The one who had woken up with the idea of incorporating enhanced eggs and seafood galore into the hors d'oeuvre course, August Belmont had also been the brains behind the open-air "mini-hot beverage terminal" that was programmed to dispense either Timbuktu espresso or Chinese Tieguauyin green tea.)

Crowned with a 26 lb. bourbon-butter basted hickory smoked rib roast (that Leonard Jerome had carved personally), the Courtyard's red oak cutting board would thus effortlessly "reel in" one William Woodward Sr. (See, this was the exact same style of beef that had been served at the post position draw.) This time around however, Woodward could also look forward to a special side saucer of Yorkshire pudding; one that was accentuated with marinade flavored pan drippings!

Of the opinion that most every mouth carried at least one sweet tooth, the "King of Wall Street" had therefore lastly equipped a roaming butler with a two hundred count platter of Chocopologie Chocolates by Knipschildt Chocolatier. (And because a Gala couldn't be labeled as such unless it had "party favors", each of these dark chocolate coated French truffles had been individually placed atop an engraved 14kt gold horseshoe which read, *"Heaven's Premier Horse Race".)*

Now by virtue of granting ten senior news journalists complete and total access to his Transcendental Gala, Leonard Jerome was preserving the "press friendly precedent" he'd set forty-eight hours prior. Presently parked down at the head of the red carpet (a.k.a., on the outer fringe of the oval), Heaven's luckiest news correspondents were consequently "rubbing elbows" with a Cigar Valet who possessed a special Spanish cedar humidor that was labeled, "*100 Count - Gurkha Grand Reserve Louis XIII Cognac Infused Cigars*". (Laughably mind you, every male in the immediate area was trying not to stare at the accompanying buxom hand maiden who'd just arrived with a basket full of "combined" red rose, Black-Eyed Susan and white carnation corsages.)

So his guests wouldn't have to limbo beneath a fiberglass barrier, the "King of Wall Street" had ordered his Grounds Crew to temporarily remove that section of outer rail which usually separated the Clubhouse's Courtyard and Jerome Park's racing surface. (Twice as large as any equine stabled along the backside, the strawberry roan Clydesdale that was hauling Samuel D. Riddle's gilded Coronation Coach ultimately pulled up to this reconfigured patch of ground at precisely 6:01 PM.)

Pretty much in one fell swoop, Mrs. Samuel D. Riddle collected both her corsage and countless compliments concerning her beaded long sleeve gold taffeta Victorian Ball gown. (Incidentally, because they were being pummeled by an endless barrage of camera flashes, those raven black Fellini tuxedos being worn by: Samuel D. Riddle, George Conway and Charlie Kurtsinger actually looked cream in color to the cocktail concierge who was on stand-by with four crystal flutes of "Shipwrecked Heidsieck".)

Though beautiful to behold, Samuel D. Riddle's Coronation Coach was immediately commandeered by the Gala's parking attendant in order to make room for William Woodward Sr.'s 17th century style Baroque Carriage. Not traditionally known for his improvisational comedic rhetoric, Willie Saunders nevertheless gave those huddled around the red carpet a good laugh when he approached August Belmont with, "Gurkha Grand Reserves huh? Gosh, you shouldn't have. Uh, so what's everyone else gonna smoke?!"

Interlude - The More the Merrier

Whereas "Caleb's Custom Invitations" had come out with an unbeatable Christmastime "Buy 25 Get 25 Free!" promotion, Leonard Jerome had gone ahead and generously invited his "regular hangout crew" (and their significant others) to the Transcendental Gala. As a result, the Connections were destined to mingle with: Colonel N. Lewis Clark (founding father of Louisville's Jockey Club, the entity responsible for instituting Churchill Downs), John Albert Morris (established Morris Park Race Course, this oval hosted both the Preakness Stakes and Belmont Stakes on the same day in 1890), Philip and Michael Dwyer (established Gravesend Racetrack, home of the Preakness Stakes from 1894 - 1908), Colonel Martin J. "Matt" Winn (formed an investment syndicate which saved Churchill Downs from extinction, likewise responsible for shrewdly marketing the Kentucky Derby and developing it into America's premier thoroughbred horse race), John Hunter and William R. Travers (established Saratoga Race Course, 1863), David Dunham Withers (thoroughbred farm proprietor and the main cultivator of New Jersey's Monmouth Park Racetrack), William "Wildman" Dennis O'Kelly (owner of Eclipse, undefeated over eighteen career starts and one of history's three "foundation thoroughbreds"), Louis Feustel and Will Harbut (Man o' War's conditioner and groom), Charles Wheatly (designer of the old Saratoga Race Course), Bill Shoemaker (supervened Eddie Arcaro as America's premier jockey, hailed for capturing eleven Triple Crown races and accumulating 8833 lifetime victories), Chic Anderson (voice of Churchill Downs and the Kentucky Derby from 1960 - 1977), Glenn Curtis and James Bright (established Hialeah Racetrack, 1921), Charles John "Chick" Lang or "Mr. Preakness" (tirelessly promoted the Triple Crown's middle jewel during his twenty-seven year tenure as Pimlico Race Course's General Manager, also rode Reigh Count (Count Fleet's sire) to victory in the 1928 Kentucky Derby), Woody Stephens (the only thoroughbred conditioner to saddle five consecutive Belmont Stakes Champions, 1982 - 1986), Jim Mckay (longtime Triple Crown analyst for NBC and co-founder of Maryland Million Day), John Gains (architect behind the Breeders' Cup World Thoroughbred Championships), Frank Y. Whiteley (conditioned Ruffian, arguably thoroughbred horse racing's greatest filly) and Frank Brunell (established the Daily Racing Form, 1894).

Albeit dead last in the receiving line (because "Deborah's Dry Cleaners" had been late in delivering Mrs. John D. Hertz's dark purple Valentino silk-georgette gown), Count Fleet's faction was still made to feel like royalty. In fact, as Mr. John D. Hertz's convertible Landau Carriage came to a halt, August Belmont approached Leonard Bernstein with, "I've heard Mrs. Hertz loves swing music so when she touches down on the red carpet, let's have the band break into "Boogie Woogie Bugle Boy"."

Seeing as how they had all "burned the midnight oil" for three solid months, the Connections naturally welcomed an occasion where they could laugh it up a bit. This was certainly the case over near the hot beverage terminal for Will Harbut had just finished telling a most tragic anecdote, one which pertained to that time where an innocent four rail fence had perished simply because it stood in-between Man o' War and a petite roan filly. Lightening the mood even further with some help from a Timbuktu espresso, Colonel "Matt" Winn contorted his face and then fooled, "If I was one of these trainers, I'd walk straight into the paddock tomorrow and force feed my horse a triple shot of this stuff!"

In the wake of receiving a text from Horace that read, **"Dinner is almost ready sir."** August Belmont started looking high and low for Jerome Park's CEO. Eventually learning (per the Gala's Barman) that his business partner was using the restroom, Belmont thereupon told the Courtyard's Cigar Valet, "Set down your humidor sir so you can help me get this flock inside!"

Home to eighteen Swarovski crystal chandeliers, the Clubhouse's Banquet Hall was also where Leonard Jerome exhibited his antique collection of equine related: ceramics, paintings, sculptures, sketches, mosaics and tapestries. (Actually given a spontaneous facelift by the "King of Wall Street" himself at around 2:00 PM, the Banquet Hall's nine "Connections' Tables" were now uniquely "color-coded" instead of just plain old white. For example, since Commander J.K.L. Ross' racing silks were black and orange, Table #1 bore: bright orange chair covers, a black table cloth, two bright orange table runners and bright orange napkins.) Of course whether their assigned seat was color-coded or not, every guest of the Transcendental Gala would ultimately sit down at a setting that was replete with: bouquets of red roses, Black-Eyed Susans and white carnations, sapphire studded 14kt gold flatware, 24kt gold rimmed crystal goblets and hand painted thoroughbred racing themed English bone china.

Once he'd returned and thanked his business partner for "taking the bull by the horns", Leonard Jerome proceeded to say "grace". Using a unified shout of "Amen!" as their cue, the Banquet Hall's Wine Stewards resultantly rushed in from all sides with their ponderous black leather tomes. (The only groom in all of Paradise who doubled as a sommelier, Toots Thompson first carefully browsed his options ahead of advocating, "Well personally gentlemen, I'd go with either the: 1787 Château Lafite, the 1978 Le Montrachet or the 1990 Romanee-Conti.")

Because the Banquet Hall also possessed two dozen roaming (and absolutely beautiful) Bar Hostesses, every guest soon owned a copy of the Transcendental Gala's "Liquor, Champagne and Beer Catalog". Rapidly receiving an order that would've cost right around $1600 at King Solomon's Tavern, Warren Wright Sr.'s crew proceeded to "quench their thirst" with: three snifters of Rémy Martin Louis XIII Cognac, two mint juleps that were made from sixteen-year old A.H. Hirsch Reserve Bourbon, a bottle of 1996 Moet et Chandon Dom Perignon Rose Champagne, four shots of Grand Marnier Cuvée 1880, five tumblers of Macallan 1926 Single Malt Scotch Whiskey, a double shot of Tres Cuatro y Cinco Extra Anejo Tequila and six bottles of Crown Ambassador Reserve Lager.

In that not everyone drank the "hard stuff", a pair of "Non-Alcoholic Beverage Attendants" would continually make the rounds behind handcarts that were stocked with: Fiuggi sparkling water, eight different blends of organic Acai berry juice, tea bags galore and various sized stainless steel coffee dispensers. (A soul who ranked coffee #2 on that list labeled, "Life's Greatest Pleasures" Leonard Jerome had thus gladly laid out the cross-dimensional tax necessary to import peerless beans from places like: Panama, Jamaica, St. Helena, Ethiopia and Indonesia.) Savvy the stuff that had shown up normally went for about fifty bucks per serving, Jean Cruget consequently indulged in a steaming hot cup of Kopi Lunak. (This unsurpassed java is brewed from partly digested coffee cherries, ones that have been plucked from feces belonging to that feline species known as the Asian Palm Civet.)

In an effort to "kill two birds with one stone" the Transcendental Gala's wait staff formally introduced themselves as they distributed the evening's fully organic salad course. Next came an opportunity to enjoy a serving of soup and as Warren Mehrtens reviewed a petite "carte du jour" card which read: *Bird's Nest, Chicken Noodle, Cream of Mushroom, Minestrone, Miso, Lobster Bisque and Shark Fin,* Table #6's well acquainted waiter informed, "Oh, and for bread sir we have: French, Italian, Cuban, sourdough, rye, wheat and pumpernickel."

Now when he saw that a great many guests were already pushing themselves away from the table, Leonard Jerome ran back to the kitchen and told his Head Chef, "I'm afraid that the Courtyard's bounty took its toll on everyone's appetite *Jehoshaphat!* We best postpone the piece de resistance."

Following an impromptu fifteen minute intermission, the Transcendental Gala's wait staff came forth from the kitchen with display trays that were flush with regal cuisine. Anxious as all get out, the Banquet Hall's Maître d' nevertheless waited until his subordinates were settled in beside their respective tables before he articulated, "Guests of the Clubhouse, it is with great pleasure that I present to you our three main entrées! First, surf and turf starring:

Highland premium angus-beef and a two pound Maine rock lobster tail. Second, grilled fat-rich Alaskan king salmon topped with: asparagus, morals and leeks. And lastly, a vegetarian medley joining: Mount Vernon winter romain, Isreali ein don cantaloupe, Tuscan black palm cabbage, cosmic purple carrots and Himalayan sikkim cucumbers."

Naturally curious as to whether or not he had succeeded, Jehoshaphat finally received his answer in the form of a text which read, "**Ten different people have asked me if they can borrow you for the next banquet they host.**"

With an immeasurable amount of satisfaction, the kitchen's Head Chef quickly wrote back, "**You just made my day sir. Hey and BTW, wait until you see these Siberian style sundaes! I went all out and used: Tahitian vanilla bean ice cream, Gold Draget truffles and chunked Amedei Porcelana chocolate!**"

As everyone tried to find room for their dessert, Leonard Jerome made the Clubhouse's renowned culinary faction come out and take a bow. Next heeding their boss' order to "take five", the Gala's gourmets hence joined in on the evening's revelry (aprons and all). In back of lavishing his help with some well deserved Shipwrecked Heidsieck, the "King of Wall Street" let loose with, "Guests of the Clubhouse, I now present to you those garments which will enswathe the winner of Heaven's Premier Horse Race!"

Although they were costumed in gold Armani tuxedos, the Banquet Hall's invading quartet was more so recognized for the long rectangular crystal case they shouldered. (To boot, an enchanting noble named *Lady Randolph Churchill* had also walked in with a shrouded package that was in the shape of a cube.) Subsequent to "killing" his third snifter of Frapin Cuvee Cognac, the "King of Wall Street" cried out, "I am proud to announce that Jerome Park will soon perpetuate one of thoroughbred horse racing's most timeless traditions! Moreover, Mr. Belmont will personally drape this novel "Tri-Floral Winner's Garland" across the withers of tomorrow's conqueror!"

So that everyone could see the treasure they bore, the Banquet Hall's "Honor Guard" quickly set their crystal case on a forty-five degree angle. Mindful that his "volume dial" only went so high, Leonard Jerome thus waited out a long chorus of "oohs" and "ahhs" before he detailed, "Ladies and gentlemen, this beautiful ten foot blanket of red roses, Black-Eyed Susans and white carnations comes to you courtesy of those talented saints who own and operate "Gideon's Greenhouse and Flower Nursery"!"

After taking a second to smell the "tip of the iceberg", August Belmont projected, "If you read the official Connections' Summit Transcript, you'll come to a place where Willie Saunders boldly suggests, *'For once, let's give the winning horse a trophy instead! Hey, how about a prize that includes a strand from each Champion's mane?!'* Well friends, for the last twelve weeks, this sector's preeminent artisan has worked tirelessly in order to perfect the "mane overlaid" victor's memento that will forever festoon the winner of Heaven's Premier Horse Race. It follows then that I now present, Lady Randolph Churchill and her utmost triumph, the "Rex Equos"!"

Understandably, Leonard Jerome welled up as his daughter unveiled that glass cube which housed Heaven's (and histories') very first "thoroughbred crown". Now since a "king" deserved both style and comfort, Lady Churchill had gone ahead and cushioned her diadem's eleven faced 22kt gold "base circlet" with a thick layer of white Alpaca fur. Wrapped with eleven commemorative name plates (starting with one that read, "*SIR BARTON*") the Rex Equos' base circlet likewise flaunted eleven 22kt gold "ascending name plate stems" that bulwarked corresponding cords of braided mane. Bending away from each other at first, these "supported braids" thereafter corporately assembled beneath a diamond and ruby trimmed 22kt gold cross which bore the phrase, "*REX EQUOS*". Intended to be translated literally, this Latin wording authoritatively conveyed, "*KING OF HORSES*".

With the evening's last major formality finally behind him, Leonard Jerome aimed to kick his Gala into high gear. First calling his symphony orchestra in from their break, the "King of Wall Street" thereupon beckoned, "Oh Lady Churchill, shall we trip the light fantastic my dear?"

Totally feeling like he had just sat down alongside his crew, Commander J.K.L Ross nevertheless owned a Supercomplication Pocket Watch that told otherwise. Following a "yawn" that could have won him an Oscar, the Transcendental Gala's initial deserter alleged, "Taking into account all I will face in just a few short hours, it's best I retire gentlemen."

Despite the fact that midnight was fast approaching, Commander J.K.L. Ross still took the time to properly thank Leonard Jerome and August Belmont for their marvelous hospitality. Subsequently bumping shoulders with Penny Chenery inside of the Clubhouse's foyer, Sir Barton's exiting owner consequently took in, "Oh excuse me Commander. I wasn't looking where I was going. You drive safe now and good luck to you tomorrow!"

In back of winking and then thinking, *"You mean good luck to us,"* Ross made his way out towards that narrow corridor which ran beneath the clubhouse turn's bowed section of temporary bleachers. Eventually surfacing just a few feet behind the gap, Jerome Park's "leading conspirator" then headed off in the direction of Equine Chateau #1. Ultimately greeted by only his shadow, Ross resultantly steamed, "Confound it! Can somebody tell me just where he is?!"

With his usual low-key demeanor, Pomeroy J. Mandalay soon casually settled beneath the warm yellow light that was being generated by Equine Chateau #1's exterior electronic lantern. Immediately discerning that he'd come into the presence of an individual who was completely and utterly paranoid, "Paradise's premier handicapper" for that reason teased, "There's no need to get your knickers twisted sir. Why I've been holed up behind that palm tree over there for a good thirty minutes!"

While he irately waggled his index finger, Ross hotly scolded, "Will you lower your voice; Jerome's night watchman is around here somewhere!"

"Uh, Jerome's night watchman is cutting Z's back behind Equine Chateau #8." Mandalay chuckled. "Yeah, don't worry Commander, there'll only be one external witness to this felony, and he can't blow the whistle on us!"

Having newly thrown his head through the top part of Equine Chateau #1's horizontally divided front door, Sir Barton continued to stare down his adulterer as he huffed, "Look Pomeroy, I'm in no mood to play games. Just take this bank envelope will you. And keep a close eye on it 'cause there's a million bucks cash in there! Now uh for the record, why don't you go ahead and recite our arrangement."

Once he had his "buy money" in hand, Heaven's highest paid errand boy submissively summarized, "I am to purchase you a one million dollar win ticket on Secretariat. If said slip is redeemed, I then become beneficiary to 10% of your net profit. Uh, and by the way Commander, if you do happen to prevail, what is our ensuing game plan?"

In the course of passing along a business card taken from "Boaz's Bed and Breakfast", Ross related, "We'll meet here at 10:00 PM, it's approximately nineteen miles due north."

"Rodger that." Mandalay replied. "Oh and sir, I know you're the type who'll cover all bases however there's no need to put a goon on retainer. Believe you me, if that big red horse delivers, then so will I."

Situated together inside a sea of empty tables, August Belmont, Eddie Arcaro, Frank Brunell and the Dwyer Brothers now lifted up five shots of sixteen-year old A.H. Hirsch Reserve Bourbon. After happily taking part in a "91.6 proof salute" aimed at Heaven's Premier Horse Race, Frank Brunell kindly revealed, "You know gentlemen, my Royal Promenade Chamber over at the "Alcázar Resort" has a gorgeous pentagon shaped poker table!"

Interlude - The Alcázar Resort

A palatial five-star 101 story property which could be seen from Jerome Park, the Alcázar Resort retained 1000 "Junior Suites" that came standard with: a canopied Tempur-Pedic California King bed, a 110" 4K television, an acrylic mineral spring Jacuzzi and a complimentary mini-bar.

Now of course if one had the means, then renting one of the Alcázar Resort's ten "Royal Promenade Chambers" was the way to go. Each equipped with its own exterior glass elevator, these three-story monarchial lairs also featured: a Eucalyptus Turkish bath, an Italian marble billiards table, a baby grand piano, two bent-grass putting greens, a walk-in cigar humidor, a burgundy felt poker table, furnished verandas, a private chef, an on-call butler and a resident massage therapist.

Within that same minute where he was finally persuaded to "ante up", August Belmont texted the Gala's parking attendant, **"Please bring my personal carriage around front sir."**

In back of packing up some firewater for the road, the Banquet Hall's remnant collectively shoved off in the direction of Leonard Jerome's capacious front porch. (Currently chit-chatting out on the Clubhouse's 14kt gold facial stairway, the "King of Wall Street" and Johnny Loftus were naturally urged to join the after party however neither man was all that interested in butting onions with the sector's most notorious card shark.) Amazed at how Citation's plastered pilot was able to keep a straight line during his descent, Jerome accordingly remarked, "That Arcaro is something else. Why with what's at stake in a few hours, you'd think he'd call it a night."

"Sleep or no sleep, "The Master" isn't going to let "Big Cy" get beat." Loftus lamented. "Yep, I hate to say it, but tomorrow's big to-do revolves around which horse fills in the exacta."

As his business partner's black Belgian carriage horse glided into motion, Jerome leaked, "Mr. Riddle basically echoed your sentiment towards the end of our little "logistical sit down". You know something though Mr.

Loftus, and believe me I'm not just saying this because you happen to be standing here. Gosh call me crazy, but I have a sneaking suspicion that Commander J.K.L. Ross is right on the cusp of his most memorable New Year's Eve ever."

Seeing as how he only had a pair of 3's to build on, Eddie Arcaro obviously knew that the correct play was to fold. Presently seated behind a small fortune, "The Master" had actually scored a brutal "KO" on the night's opening hand courtesy of a queen-high flush however since only cultured gentlemen inhabited the room, there were no hard feelings. (As a matter of fact, a bone-weary August Belmont had been more than happy to trade his "buy-in" for a date with Frank Brunell's leased Tempur-Pedic California King bed.)

Ultimately completing his shuffle for the evening's final hand of five card draw at 6:07 AM, Eddie Arcaro had thereupon dealt clockwise (first to one Philip J. Dwyer). Quick to "lead out" with a crisp $50 bill, Dwyer's aggressive opening bet had already been matched dollar for dollar by the player seated in third position (a.k.a., Frank Brunell). Parked on "the dealer's" right hand side, Michael F. Dwyer now wisely conceded both his assortment of "rags" and his $10 ante yet for some strange reason; "The Master" just couldn't get away from his "treys". Subsequent to boosting the kitty with yet another portrait of *Ulysses S. Grant*, Arcaro frankly disclosed, "I pretty sure I'm behind gentlemen but hey, I'm not about to sit out the evening's last dance."

Soon called on to "discard", Philip J. Dwyer consequently threw one of his Tally-ho Circle Back squares into the muck. Eventually mirroring Frank Brunell's ensuing move, "The Master" then "reloaded" the table as he aired, "One for Phil, three for Frank and dealer takes three as well gentlemen."

That player whom the "action was now on", Philip J. Dwyer thus elected to wager a pair of slightly worn c-notes. Apparently in it for the long haul, Frank Brunell quickly counted out $1200 in advance of particularizing, "I'll raise you $1000 sir."

Because he had spotted a small "tell", Eddie Arcaro was fairly confident that Philip J. Dwyer had attempted to "buy" the pot. On the other hand, it appeared that Brunell definitely had the goods however this didn't stop "The Master" from spouting, "I re-raise gentlemen. Call the $1200, and make it another $2000."

Behind saying, "adios" to his busted straight, Philip J. Dywer turned an enquiring eye towards Frank Brunell. Concernedly sighing, "Man if this doesn't hold up," as he parted with twenty "Benjamins", the father of The Daily Racing Form next added, "Laying this hand down would be maniacal Eddie. Yup, if you beat me, I can live with it."

Even though he had miraculously picked up three aces, Eddie Arcaro's full house looked downright paltry aside of four tens. Needing both hands to do so, Frank Brunell first raked in a pot worth exactly $6790 before he sincerely sighed, "My apologies Eddie. That's the worst cooler I have ever seen."

Cognizant it was now his turn to be gracious, "The Master" therefore shook hands and then quoted, "Like Mr. Belmont said Frank, 'you win some, you lose some.' Hey and since your bankroll is now nice and healthy, let me tell you about a hot 2-1 tip that a reliable jockey gave me!"

Chapter 18 - Heaven's Premier Horse Race

Settled high above the backstretch in the heart of Bleacher Section #24, Ron Turcotte's shining eyes were presently fixated on that which monopolized the horizon. (Resplendently draped in dawn's psychedelic aurora, Jerome Park's Main Grandstand now also seemed to own a tangible voice, one which thunderously trumpeted glad tidings to each and every haloed member of Horse Racing Nation.)

Eventually dropping down to one knee, Meadow Farms' second most valuable commodity next went to thanking God for shepherding him through what had been a terribly trying fourteen week season. (See, in addition to shouldering his organization's great expectations, Turcotte had likewise endured a ridiculously dour nutritional regiment. ...And actually if you want the truth, Secretariat's pious pilot had only "made his riding weight" because he'd somehow stuck to a strict ninety day "no sugar and low carb diet". ...Yes, even throughout the course of Leonard Jerome's Transcendental Gala!)

Following a few more minutes of quiet time with the Lord, Ron Turcotte set out to inspect "the stadium turf". Cognizant this would be more than just a five minute chore, "Big Red's" right hand man hence dredged up Lucien Laurin's contact number and then texted, **"Let's push our breakfast meeting back to 7:45. I want to walk the strip to see if those showers we had this morning created any spongy patches."**

      As he grabbed hold of his upstairs veranda's wrought iron railing, Leonard Jerome also bravely faced up to the day's first conundrum. Well aware that his worn out staff was still breaking down the banquet hall, the "King of Wall Street" consequently decided to dial "1-800-GRUB-2GO" however right as the phone rang, Jehoshaphat rolled in with: a pot of Costa-Rican coffee, two strawberry topped Belgium waffles and three crisp strips of apple wood bacon.

Interlude - An Indispensible Supporting Cast

      *Even though it was closed to the public on "race day" until the hour of 10:00 AM, Heaven's principal sports palace was anything but dormant. (Hired way back on November 19th during a universally advertised on-site job fair, Jerome Park's ponderous "Operations Staff" had actually reported in for work at the midpoint of Heaven's "fourth watch" (4:30 AM).) Now because he'd printed a "want-ad" which had included "***Bonuses paid for experience!***", the "King of Wall Street" was currently seated above a five million dollar team of: admission attendants, parking valets, program vendors, pari-mutuel tellers, A/V technicians, culinary savants, ushers, outriders, V.I.P box butlers, bartenders,* *sanitation engineers, waitresses, merchandise retailers, floor managers and departmental directors.*

In-between chewing and reflecting on the Transcendental Gala, Jerome casually asked his Head Chef, "Hey, by the way, at what time did Mr. Belmont get home?"

While he kept his head down, Jehoshaphat reluctantly passed along, "Well, Mr. Brunell carried him up the front steps a little after 6:30 AM sir. Yeah, and it's probably not my place to say but, it does appear that your partner's impromptu gallivanting took its toll."

With quite a worried face, the veranda's viceroy immediately took off down that winding corridor which led towards August Belmont's vaulted bedchamber. Soon shooing away the shower steam that had slid out from beneath his business partner's bathroom door, the "King of Wall Street" then beckoned, "Good morning there lad! I say, the big day is finally upon us!"

Ultimately thrown into a complete panic by "the sound of silence", Jerome as a result shouted, "August! August! Answer me old boy! Are you conscious sir?!"

Compliments of a kisser that was buried beneath a hot shower, Belmont languidly groaned, "Just barely Leonard, just barely. Uh, be a good fellow and find me some Tylenol will you?!"

"O.K., however a hangover is best combated with plenty of water so don't neglect your fluids!" Jerome cried.

"Oh and hey, don't stay in there all day! I want to be down near the turnstiles when we open!"

In back of straightening up like a barnyard rooster, Belmont blared, "In all our years together have I ever once kept you waiting Leonard?! Ugh, I'll be in the Courtyard ready to go at five 'till ten, just like we planned!"

Once he was reacquainted with his breakfast plate, Jerome politely asked, "Do you have a minute to fetch Mr. Belmont some Tylenol and a few bottles of spring water?"

"Surely, and I'll throw in a light breakfast too." Jehoshaphat sighed. "Oh and by the way sir, your grooming attendant came by looking for you. She's waiting in the downstairs salon with that new straight razor that Mr. Wheatly gave you for Christmas."

Growing at a rate of ten feet per second, the queue to get into Leonard Jerome's empire was currently wrapping itself around the front of Bathsheba's Bistro. Similarly, there had also been a population boom inside of the far reaching plain that was directly behind shed row. Spread out like locusts across this supplementary parking area, Jerome Park's broad band of tailgaters were presently poised to integrate over one million pounds of charcoal and enough chow to feed a small commonwealth.

Strolling into public view at exactly 10:00 AM, Leonard Jerome and August Belmont thereupon shook hands with the first one thousand saints who came through the turnstiles. Now even though post time was still 480 minutes away, Horse Racing Nation didn't have to worry about succumbing to severe boredom. (See, on top of organizing a legendary Transcendental Gala Dinner, Jerome Park's two primary tenants had also intricately coordinated a property wide race day "Fan Festival".)

Set up a stone's throw from the turnstiles, Jerome's Park's outdoor "Turf Bookstore" retained an endless array of racing related: biographies, novels, magazines, photographic anthologies and of course, the official 111 page full color program for Heaven's Premier Horse Race. Retailing at its $7.50 production cost, this publication's front cover (which had been expertly designed by Lady Randolph Churchill) fantastically featured a rearing thoroughbred who was bedecked in both the Tri-Floral Winner's Garland and the Rex Equos. Additionally, program purchasers would also acquire: three months worth of workout summaries, lifetime past performances, behind the scenes photographs, connection profiles and of course, Leonard Jerome's very own pari-mutual commentary!

Camped on the apron just left of the Winner's Enclosure, Leonard Jerome's "Leonard Bernstein led" ninety-nine piece symphony orchestra was scheduled to perform a: 10:00 AM, 12:00 PM, 2:00 PM and a 4:00 PM set. Moreover, musically inclined callers who wished to "sit in" were free to sign-out any of those instruments that the "King of Wall Street" had rented from "Jubal's Jazz Outlet". (Famous because they would restring any angelic harp (no matter the size) for only $19.99, Paradise's principal music emporium had actually also sent over a volunteer bugler who would spend his day teaching those interested how to play "Call to the Post".)

212

After he'd said goodnight to Johnny Loftus, the "King of Wall Street" had helped Horace move some of the Clubhouse's choice collectables into the Main Grandstand's upper west corridor. Owning a Masters Degree in Art History from Columbia University, Horace for that reason was scheduled to give both a 12:30 PM and a 2:30 PM lecture in front of a priceless sampling of equine related: ceramics, paintings, sculptures, sketches, mosaics and tapestries.

Since a superabundance of affordable themed merchandise waited in the wings, Horse Racing Nation could count on going souvenir crazy. In fact for only $10.00, fans could outfit themselves in a cotton t-shirt that said, **"JEROME PARK est. 1866"** and an adjustable baseball hat which read, *"Heaven's Premier Horse Race"*. Furthermore, there was certainly no shortage of themed: pennants, balloons, postcards, coffee mugs, polo knits, key chains, foam fingers, jackets, plush equines, umbrellas or barkers who yelled things like, "Get your War Admiral lunch-boxes here! Get your Sir Barton beach towels here!"

For obvious reasons, Jerome Park's paddock was picked as the backdrop for the day's 1:00 PM to 4:00 PM "Legend's Meet and Greet". Incredibly mind you, anyone who stopped by would get to pet and say, "Hi" to: *Seabiscuit, Nashua, Kelso, Man o' War, John Henry, Forego, Native Dancer, Dr. Fager, Ruffian, Swaps* and *Barbaro*! (Oh yeah, and along with getting their "celebrity fix", guests would also return to their seats with a complimentary 8x10 group photo of these equine immortals.)

Without any hesitation, Leonard Jerome had gone ahead and let Jehoshaphat contract all of his race day catering needs. Operating out of a gazebo that was opposite

213

the Turf Bookstore, "Grill Masters Inc." was the place for: 100% Angus Beef hamburgers, Philly cheese steaks, filler-free foot long hot dogs and loaded potato skins. Of course for those counting calories, the obvious choice would be "Brunch Bonanza" (i.e., that round rotunda behind the far turn where patrons could obtain different kinds of: soups, salads, fruit medleys, spinach dips, hummus trays, protein shakes and vegetable smoothies). Sure to be a favorite among those who preferred down home cooking, "Aunt Bessie's Soul Food Truck" was currently advertising a dinner comprised of: baby back ribs, fried chicken, grilled fish, pig's feet, pork-jowl bacon, hog maw, oxtails, black eyed peas, coleslaw, cornbread and iced tea for only $17.99. Centrally set on the infield beneath a neon sign that read, "FOOD FANTASY INC." Jerome Park's best sustenance station wasn't all that cheap, however neither was the wholesale price of: Sterlet caviar, escargot, pheasant, veal, duck, buffalo, camel, and Blue Whale blubber.

Although he had long known the exact locale of Jerome Park's Jockeys' Room (in-between Equine Chateau #1 and the paddock), this was actually the first time that Steve Cauthen had done any internal sightseeing. Now despite the fact that he was already seriously late for his 12:15 PM in-house sports massage appointment, "The Kid" purposefully took a detour past Dressing Room #11 in order to thank the valet who was carefully readying his: silks, saddle, helmet, goggles, riding boots and whipping baton. (Later on of course, Cauthen would come to find out that his private "3/4 bathroom" contained all sorts of goodies like: oatmeal body wash, grape seed oil shampoo, coconut cream conditioner, an electronic tooth brush, whitening toothpaste, mint flavored waxed floss, melon extract mouthwash, cedar wood and juniper deodorant, four Turkish bath towels, an Egyptian cotton robe, a cologne turntable, sandalwood shaving cream and a 10kt gold gripped titanium blade safety razor.)

Since Leonard Jerome had thoughtfully decided to mail out eleven "suggestion cards", the Jockeys' Room's "Common Area" bore much more than just your usual physical therapy and warm up equipment. (Alas, Eddie Arcaro had only been kidding when he wrote down: *wall mounted 160' 4K television, eleven-piece red leather sectional sofa, air hockey table, pinball machine, nine foot billiards table, Pac-Man arcade game, Snoopy snow cone maker, dart board, mini-basketball hoop and a skee-ball machine.*)

In order to take his mind off all "the pressure" he was feeling, Steve Cauthen promptly lent an ear to Common Area's 160' 4K television. (Airing live from inside Jerome Park's Main Grandstand, a trio of handicappers employed by the "Eternity Broadcast Network" were currently discussing the following "updated" prices: #1 - Sir Barton 26/1, #2 - Whirlaway 17/1, #3 - Omaha 12/1, #4 - Citation 2/1, #5 - Gallant Fox 7/1, #6 - Secretariat 2/1, #7 - Assault 11/1,

#8 - Seattle Slew 5/1, #9 - Affirmed 12/1, #10 - Count Fleet 32/1, #11 - War Admiral 11/1.)

Irked because his two associates had conservatively touted Secretariat and Citation, EBN's lead correspondent subsequently spouted, "Truthfully, I'm stunned gentlemen. I mean here we have the deepest field of Champion thoroughbreds ever assembled and yet you're both willing to settle for 2-1 odds!"

Finally rubbed into a sort of trance (thanks to a few squarely smacked pressure points), Steve Cauthen thus "hopped out of his skin" when he abruptly heard, "Man where's the remote?! These clowns are giving me a headache!"

As he pointed towards the Common Area's glass coffee table, "The Kid" asked, "Hey speaking of pain man, how's that busted finger doing?"

Paying his splint no mind, Al Snider instead brought up, "Man my shoulder is the real problem. When Whirlaway dumped me it like got out of whack."

First putting his head back down, Cauthen then counseled, "Have your assigned masseuse treat it with some tiger balm. By post time it'll be good as new."

"Hey thanks, I'll do that." Snider replied. "First though, I want to drop in on Whirlaway. With the Gala and all, I didn't get a chance to spend any time with him yesterday."

Presently being "chopped" across the lower back, "The Kid" consequently stuttered, "Wow, now that was a party! Gosh, can you imagine what that spread must've cost?!"

While he shook his head, the Common Area's vertical pilot remarked, "I'll tell you, Mr. Jerome's net worth took a big hit just on account of Arcaro being there! Why that whippersnapper put away one of everything in the courtyard plus three courses of surf and turf!"

"Ha! That's not all he put away!" Cauthen amusedly cackled.

Since his pal had "gone there", Snider proceeded to slap on, "I know right. Unfortunately for us, "The Master" is rumored to be 31 for 31 when riding with a hangover."

Sent from his Senior Admissions Director's phone at 4:14 PM, Leonard Jerome's latest text message read, "**FYI, your racetrack stands at 100% capacity.**" In the course of thinking, *"Mm, not quite,"* the "King of Wall Street" hastily wrote back, "**Disable all turnstiles and break the bad news to those waiting in the standby queue.**"

Fed up with "running on fumes", August Belmont had therefore gone back to the Clubhouse in order to brew a double espresso. Actually never getting his cup of jo, Belmont nevertheless "grew wings" when Leonard Jerome called up to inform, "An angelic entourage just enveloped Section 2A. Uh, that means *He's* like one minute away!"

A literal "Eden" that was located on the Main Grandstand's second level, Section 2A contained: 100 Luxury Tenements, 9 Owners' Boxes and one Sovereign Imperial Suite that was directly across from the finish line. Reserved for select V.I.P's (like King Solomon) and those who'd attended the Transcendental Gala, Section 2A's Luxury Tenements had been designed to include: purple shag carpeting, seven gold leather recliners, a 70" 4K viewing monitor, seven solid pearl end tables, a fully stocked corner bar, seven programs autographed by each participating Connection, seven pairs of high powered 14kt gold binoculars, a personal chef and one designated "box butler". (With reference to the Owners' Boxes, well, they basically mirrored the Luxury Tenements except that they also had foot Jacuzzis.)

Easily the best seat in the house (since it'd been built on a seven square meter platform that extended out from the Main Grandstand's center patio), Section 2A's Sovereign Imperial Suite featured: a 24kt gold diamond encrusted throne, plenty of fresh baked lightly salted matzah, an endless assortment of vestal wines and a real-life African Lion footstool.

A sight to see as it landed on the apron, *Jesus Christ's* blazing chariot derived its horsepower from seven fiery winged-stallions. Genuflecting prior to showing the *"King of Kings"* His throne, Leonard Jerome next leaned over and whispered, "August my man, we owe *Daniel* big time for loaning us that lion."

Inside of that exact moment where he was finally able to take a deep breath, the "King of Wall Street" fielded a frantic phone call from his Pari-Mutual Manager. Quickly stooping down below the ambient noise so he could hear, Section 2A's "go-to guy" subsequently absorbed, "I'm terribly sorry to bother you sir, but *William Henry Vanderbilt* is down here trying to pass a personal check for $100,000!"

As he made a break for the Main Grandstand's center circular staircase, Jerome huffed, "That's my old business partner's eldest son for you, just loves pushing the envelope! O.K *Caalum*, I'll be right down."

Not more than one minute after he'd explained, "Sorry William, but if I do this for you I'll have to do it for everybody," the "King of Wall Street" coincidently crossed paths with none other than *Commodore Cornelius Vanderbilt*. First tipping his top hat towards the soul who had helped finance his Earthly railroad empire, the good Commodore then came out with, "Please pardon that cuckoo child of mine Leonard, he should know better. Oh, and wish me luck. See, I'll be a couple hundred thousand richer if Citation lives up to my expectations."

With quite the candid look, Jerome stated, "I wish luck to every punter on the premises today Cornelius, uh, whether they are staking six figures or only six dollars. Now if you'll excuse me, I'm headed behind-the-scenes for a quick conference concerning the current betting handle."

For whatever reason, the "King of Wall Street" would always whistle "Camptown Races" whenever he looked at any type of financial summary (and today was no exception). Enjoying the music from behind a brass desk plate that read, **"Pari-Mutual Manager"** Caalum courteously gave his boss a minute before he carried on with, "Gosh, nearly half a billion in action and there's still eighty-seven minutes left until post time! Oh yeah, and congratulations on winning our bet sir. Man, I just never thought that we would take in over a million bucks worth of silver bullion!"

Once he'd flipped over the spreadsheet that was in his hand, Jerome sermonized, "If this business has taught me anything sir, it's that an insolvent horseplayer will raise their stake by any means necessary. Why just pick up the Eternity Times' morning edition if you don't believe me. There's an editorial inside talking about how punters have pawned everything from a 16 oz. black pearl to an original *Picasso* painting!"

While he tried not to laugh, Caalum clued in, "One of my tellers showed me that article. I also read the piece that predicted how this race will easily be the most watched sporting event in television history!"

220

In spite of the reflection that was in Dressing Room #8's full length mirror, Eddie Arcaro simply couldn't believe that he was once again wearing those throw back "candy red silks" that were so famously associated with Calumet Farms. Ultimately invited into the Jockeys' Room's jammed packed Common Area at 5:15 PM, "The Master" then heard August Belmont generally announce, "O.K. riders listen up! Seeing as how he desires a commemorative group photo, Mr. Jerome has requested that you congregate along the front edge of Equine Chateau #1's foraging field at 5:35 PM! Afterwards, you are free to pursue the paddock and..."

Following an inquisitive shrug that was aimed at the Jockeys' Room's reverberating doorbell, Belmont stammered, "Who in the world could that... Uh, just sit tight for a moment gentlemen."

Soon standing in the middle of the Common Area, *John the Apostle* carried on until Johnny Longden interrupted, "Please stop apologizing sir. If you felt led to come in here and bless us, then by all means proceed."

When he was finished speaking out the prayer of protection that had been placed in his heart, Paradise's predominant revelator reported, "Please look past my hasty departure men. If I hurry, I'll also be able to lay hands on those who will carry you into battle."

Shortly after they were "lifted up", the entrants for Heaven's Premier Horse Race were brought out onto shed row by their respective Connections. Currently standing in the middle of Equine Chateau #6's foraging field with a megaphone he'd borrowed from the Clubhouse, Leonard Jerome was thus heard loud and clear as he blazoned, "Attention all owners, conditioners and grooms! The time is now exactly 5:28 PM! In approximately two minutes, a paddock walkover led by Mr. Louis Wolfson's troop will commence! For everyone's safety, please remain in single file as you thread the gap and swing onto the backstretch. Also, please be aware that after your Champions exit the paddock for the post parade, a police escort will immediately begin the process of transitioning you over to the Main Grandstand! Good luck to all and enjoy the race!"

Amid a thousand potential distractions, Pomeroy J. Mandalay somehow managed to equally split his attention between Secretariat's 9/5 tote odds and a tightly gripped alligator skin briefcase that contained $1,300,000. Now even though Big Red's current price translated into a risk-free shot at $180,000, "Paradise's premier handicapper" couldn't see past the one glaring drawback that was associated with Commander J.K.L. Ross' sponsored "free roll" (i.e., a deep-seated suspicion that Citation would ultimately prove to be Heaven's fastest racehorse).

In the aftermath of hearing, "Step right up, no wait," Mandalay opened his reptilian satchel atop the frosted marble counter that trimmed Pari-Mutual Window #38. "All-

222

business" as he slid ten uncirculated $100,000 bills beneath his agent's polished brass cage, Commander J.K.L. Ross' minion subsequently commented, "Such a shame, notes as lovely as those being scarred by a counterfeit pen. Anyway when you can get around to it, I'll take one million dollars on #6 to win."

Once he had checked (and re-checked) his mainstay's ticket for accuracy, Mandalay started envisioning the white security envelope that was stashed in the side pocket of his briefcase. Finally snapped out of his trance by the query of, "Uh, will there be anything else sir?" Pari-Mutual Window #38's mulling client thereafter articulated, "Oh sorry, I was just deciding whether or not to hedge my bet. Mm yeah, go ahead and give me $300,000 on #4 to win as well."

In spite of everything that Luxury Tenement #36 had to offer, William R. Travers had remained a visual slave to Jerome Park's gap. (See, because Travers owned a tote-ticket that read, "**$5000 SHOW 9**" he was therefore anxious to see how Affirmed would conduct himself as he "came through the ropes".) Soon led onto the backstretch in front of 575,000 hysterical "turf-freaks", Louis Wolfon's heavyweight ultimately (and surprisingly) responded by letting out a yawn that would have made *Rip Van Winkle* proud.

Because there was so much forethought aimed at who was next in the arrival queue, Seattle Slew came through the gap thinking, *"Hey, am I invisible or something?!"* On the contrary, Secretariat's appearance "brought down the house" to the extent that EBN's lead commentator went on to say, "It sounds like Chapter 11 filings will reach an all-time high if "Big Red" doesn't pull this thing off boys!"

Physically abandoning the backside as Citation went onstage, Leonard Jerome thereupon scurried to join August Belmont inside the Stewards' Chamber (a.k.a., that small-scale unmarked "Judge's Booth" which sat atop the Main Grandstand's roof). Incidentally, since it was universally understood that he and Belmont would have the final say concerning any "claim of foul", the "King of Wall Street" had thus repeatedly mentioned, "I keep praying that our winner doesn't somehow impede any of his rivals along the way August. A disqualification, no matter how justified, would put a tremendous damper on things."

Having successfully applied for the job of "Paddock Judge" at Jerome Park's November 19th job fair, Colonel Matt Winn was hence responsible for checking each entrant into their designated saddling enclosure. Looking somewhat "star-struck" as he handed Jimmy Jones a gold saddle cloth that was embroidered with the number "**4**", Colonel Winn next glanced both ways before he quietly disclosed,

"Confidentially sir, I think that your racer is the class of this field."

One who had loudly echoed Winn's sentiment all afternoon, Salbatore Zarcos was presently in the middle of draining his eighth chalice of red "extra fruity" sangria. Reclining alongside his three brothers in Section 2B, Jerome Park's smuggest Spaniard went right on obnoxiously touting Citation until one *Señor Carlos Zarcos* posed, "Answer me this Salbatore, if "Big Cy" can't lose, then why is your wallet splitting at the seams?!"

In back of surrendering his boa constrictor skin billfold to his youngest sibling, Salbatore Zarcos slurred, "There is $250,000 in there boy. Go buy me a ticket for that amount on #4 to win!"

Given that he was texting August Belmont, **"2 min. away"** Leonard Jerome very nearly trampled a soft pretzel vendor as he darted up the Main Grandstand's center circular staircase. Ultimately delayed in getting to his destination because he had to hurdle fifty-five rooftop television cameras, the "King of Wall Street" resultantly entered the Stewards' Chamber to the tune of, "Well there you are! Quick now chap, come look! Your daughter and her four deputies are bringing the Tri-Floral Winner's Garland and the Rex Equos into the Winner's Enclosure!"

Wishing the best to one another once they were on the business side of the paddock's 14kt gold fence, Jerome Park's jockey colony had then quickly fanned out towards their respective "families". Currently unable to hear over the cheers that were dousing those who'd been saddled, Warren Mehrtens consequently reached for Max Hirsch's touch screen tablet so he could type, **"If you have any last second instructions for me, write them out on this."**

A direct result of the concentrated energy that was swirling around him, Whirlaway suddenly began drooling and throwing his head from side to side. Evidenced by the way he was kicking his paddock stall's rear partition, Count Fleet also showed himself to be a "hair fidgety". Another whose vibes were less than encouraging, Omaha had actually produced a layer of sweat that caused Willie Saunders to wonder, *"Man, did someone take a fire hose to him?"*

In the wake of being implored upon by Colonel Matt Winn, the paddock's "perimeter groupies" respectfully piped down. Now afforded the opportunity to execute his last official duty, Winn therefore stuffed his lungs so he could relay, "Riders up!"

After they were given a "leg up", Jerome Park's jockey colony immediately went into "carousel mode" atop the paddock's 14kt gold brick walking ring. Currently being bombarded by this gilt road's bright reflection, Adelphia Armour accordingly dug out the tortoise shell spectacle case that was in her Gucci handbag. (Complemented earlier on her red ruffled wide brimmed hat, Section 1C's prettiest punter now likewise took in, "Girlfriend! You must tell me where you got your Bvlgari Parentesi sunglasses!")

Prompted by Leonard Bernstein at 5:45 PM, the "King of Wall Street's" ninety-nine piece symphony orchestra thereupon performed a dramatic rendition of "Call to the Post". Plainly hearing that it was time to lead the field onto the track, Johnny Loftus now went and did just that (albeit with a pair of hands that trembled uncontrollably). Immediately moving in as the post parade's caboose (a.k.a., War Admiral) moved out, the paddock's police squad soon after heard their 6'6" sergeant shout, "No time to waste now boys! Let's gather these folks up and get them to their seats!"

Despite being best known for a unique comparison he'd made during the 1973 Belmont Stakes, Chic Anderson's appointment to call Heaven's Premier Horse Race wasn't based on the verbiage, *"He (Secretariat) is moving like a tremendous machine!"* Truth be told, Leonard Jerome had been won over by a gleaming résumé that listed prosperous partnerships with entities like: Churchill Downs, Belmont Park, Aqueduct Racetrack, Santa Anita Park, Oaklawn Park, Arlington Park, Ak-Sar-Ben Racetrack and Ellis Park.

Sitting next door to the Stewards' Chamber inside of Jerome Park's Announcer's Booth, Chic Anderson was currently preoccupied with the far turn's twenty-two part bilateral counter-clockwise procession (each of the day's entrants naturally had their own individual outrider). Deeming that it was the right time to un-mute his microphone, Anderson thus "flipped the switch" and then decorously transmitted, "Ladies and gentlemen, your attention please! On behalf of Mr. Leonard Walter Jerome, Mr. August Belmont Sr. and those Connections intimately associated with eternity's eleven Triple Crown Champions, I hereby welcome you to Jerome Park, site of Heaven's Premier Horse Race!"

As the outside noise level fell back below eighty decibels, "the voice of Jerome Park" continued, "Ladies and gentlemen, for generations, the songs: "My Old Kentucky Home", "Maryland my Maryland" and "New York New York" have been synonymous with Thoroughbred Horse Racing's Triple Crown Series. Responsible for birthing "My Old Kentucky Home" back in 1852, the great *Stephen Foster* has now furthered his legacy by blending the Triple Crown's three traditional hymns into what will be today's entrance anthem. So with that said, please turn your attention towards Jerome Park's symphony orchestra as Mr. Foster guest conducts, "A Triple Crown Trilogy". Finally, Mr. Jerome kindly asks that all patrons sing along using those lyrics found on page 3 of today's race program."

Lasting exactly three minutes, Horse Racing Nation's show of solidarity ultimately wrapped up just as the strip's bilateral counter-clockwise procession reached the three-sixteenths pole. Now needing to wipe his eyes, Chic Anderson also took a quick sip of water before he publicized, "Ladies and gentlemen, here is your post parade for Heaven's Premier Horse Race!

...Leading off in post position #1 is Sir Barton! Owned by the honorable Commander J.K.L. Ross, this field's "elder statesman" is trained by H.G. Bedwell and will be ridden today by Johnny Loftus.

Hailing from Lexington, Kentucky's illustrious Calumet Farms, Whirlaway will break from post #2! Entered by one Warren Wright Sr., "Mr. Longtail" owes his conditioning to six-time Kentucky Derby winning trainer Ben Jones. Finally making his long awaited come back, your jockey is today's "sentimental favorite", the one and only Al Snider.

Omaha has a confirmed reservation with post #3! Property of Belair Stud CEO William Woodward Sr., the aptly nicknamed "Belair Bullet" is trained by legendary horseman James Fitzsimmons! Willie "Smokey" Saunders occupies the driver's seat.

Another who is coming to you courtesy of Calumet Farms, Citation is set to load into post #4! The prized possession of Warren Wright Sr. and readied by Jimmy Jones, "Big Cy's" jockey is none other than "The Master", Eddie Arcaro.

Post #5 features Gallant Fox! Also prepped for today's contest by James Fitzsimmons, the second half of William Woodward Sr.'s potent squadron will receive his instructions via the sublime Earl Sande.

The pride of Meadow Stables and your current betting favorite, Secretariat is slated to originate from post #6! Retained by Penny Chenery and trained by Lucien Laurin, "Big Red" will have regular rider Ron Turcotte calling the shots.

Set on a collision course with post #7 is the state of Texas' very own Assault! Here courtesy of Robert J. Kleberg, the "Club Footed Comet" has one Max Hirsch to thank for his prime physique. Warren Mehrtens gets the call.

Seattle Slew is primed to be placed into post #8! Sent out by Mickey and Karen Taylor, thoroughbred racing's tenth Triple Crown Champion has been prepared for his biggest challenge to date by one Billy Turner. Monsieur Jean Cruget is in the irons.

A native of Louis Wolfson's Harbor View Farm, Affirmed will leave from post #9! Trained up to Heaven's Premier Horse Race under the watchful eye of Laz Barerra, this field's youngest participant is of course paired with rider, and hero, Steve Cauthen, a.k.a., "The Kid".

Post #10 belongs to that Champion we know as Count Fleet! Stoner Creek Stud Farm's favorite son work's exclusively for Mrs. John D. Hertz and owes his physical fettle to Don Cameron. Johnny Longden sits topside.

Rounding out the field in post #11 is the wieldy War Admiral! Owned by Samuel D. Riddle and trained by George Conway, Man o' War's most renowned progeny is set up with the "chilly" Charlie Kurtsinger at the controls."

Awarded the position of "Head Starter" by the "King of Wall Street", Chick Lang was currently looking at the back end of Jerome Park's eleven-stall 14kt gold starting gate. First telling his twenty-two person "gate crew" to gather in around him, "Mr. Preakness" then emphasized, "Don't forget that we're gonna deal with Riddle's delinquent first men!

And hey, if *Harley* and *Horatio* can't get that lout to load, then it's all hands on deck!"

While he had been "as cool as a cucumber" inside of the paddock, Assault was anything but during his pre-race warm up. Initially boomeranging all over the place, the "Club Footed Comet" then performed a high "bunny hop" right as Leonard Jerome said, "Jeepers August, Kleberg's boy looks worse than: Whirlaway, Count Fleet and Omaha combined."

Now unlike the strip's "disquieted quartet", Secretariat, Citation, Seattle Slew and Gallant Fox definitely had their game faces on. Admittedly enamored with these "A-listers", August Belmont thus passionately pointed with his binoculars while he digressed, "Yeah well the four favorites look phenomenal! You know frankly Leonard; I think anyone who purchased a 4-5-6-8 superfecta box has good reason to be encouraged!"

One of three sending "mixed signals", Sir Barton indeed had himself some happy feet however H.G. Bedwell was truly concerned about his horse's burbling brow sweat (especially since it was only 64 degrees outside). Mostly happy with how Affirmed felt, Steve Cauthen nevertheless knew that Louis Wolfson's level headed Champion usually never jumped shadows. Currently cantering clockwise around the clubhouse turn, War Admiral definitely had "energy to burn" yet this one was also right on the brink of becoming what you'd call "a little too juiced up".

On the heels of getting good and loose, the field for Heaven's Premier Horse Race reconvened with their outriders in front of the finish line. Quick to form a bilateral column that faced Jerome Park's chute, Sir Barton and company subsequently began their "approach" beneath an exceptionally beautiful edition of dusk. (Consisting of hues akin to gold, plum, rust and scarlet, Jerome Park's present iridescent overlay had actually come courtesy of a certain deity who was seated in Section 2A.)

As he came around the back of Leonard Jerome's prized eleven-stall 14kt gold starting gate, War Admiral was instantly surrounded. Outfitted in ball-caps that read, **"Assistant Starter Stall #11"** Harley and Horatio continued with their cautious advance until Charlie Kurtsinger furiously snapped, "I ain't puttin' up with your tomfoolery today boy! Now get moving!"

Lifting his head once War Admiral was safely under lock and key, George Conway thereafter tittered, "See Mr. Riddle, who says that prayer doesn't work?"

Because it appeared that his crew had things well under control, Chick Lang went and ducked beneath that section of rail which fringed the inside of Jerome Park's harrowed chute. Already in possession of the starting gate's remote control release buzzer, "Mr. Preakness" continued his ascent up the "Starter's Platform's" rear stairwell as Chic Anderson soberly announced, "Sir Barton goes in without incident. Next we have Whirlaway, followed by Omaha…"

Coming mildly unglued for a moment as he walked into stall #4, Citation in turn spooked the living daylights out of Gallant Fox. Somehow able to load in his mount regardless, the "Fox of Belair's" jockey resultantly heard "the voice of Jerome Park" compliment, "Kudos to Sande for maintaining his composure. Secretariat now moves forward, Assault restlessly slides in aside of that one…"

After he was tied in with those who could only sit and wait, Jean Cruget passed the time by estimating the gold content value of stall #8. Unhesitatingly doing the right thing as soon as Steve Cauthen showed up, Seattle Slew's considerate pilot pointed and then particularized, "Hey kid, there's a small piece of lint or something just above Affirmed's left eye."

Surprising everyone with his reluctance to load, Count Fleet in fact reared up on his hind legs before he finally completed the line up at exactly 18 seconds until post time. Established 42 seconds prior at 5:59 PM, the closing pari-mutual prices for Heaven's Premier Horse Race wound up being: #1 - Sir Barton 27/1, #2 - Whirlaway 16/1, #3 - Omaha 12/1, #4 - Citation 2/1, #5 - Gallant Fox 8/1, #6 - Secretariat 9/5, #7 - Assault 11/1, #8 - Seattle Slew 9/2, #9 - Affirmed 9/1, #10 - Count Fleet 31/1, #11 - War Admiral 10/1.

Presently perched on stall #11's right partition, Horatio finally got War Admiral to straighten his head out. First double-checking that the rest of the field was still ready to go, Chick Lang next aimed his "**JP**" embroidered starter's flag directly at Jesus Christ's raised right hand. Given the "green light" by the *Son of God* right as Jerome Park's turquoise clock tower tolled 6:00 PM, "Mr. Preakness" thereupon initiated the most anticipated equine engagement of all time.

In back of perfectly timing the break, Charlie Kurtsinger ambitiously tried to merge War Admiral across ten lanes of long-legged traffic. (Unfortunately, not every neighbor had gone and copied Count Fleet's "Galápagos tortoise like" launch.) Now owning an easy decision (because both Affirmed and Seattle Slew were showing crazy early speed), Johnny Longden consequently wrangled his "tardy starter" back (in preference of burning up the "horsepower" it would take to go after the lead).

An equine who desperately wanted out of stall #7, Assault therefore broke completely crossways. Instantly ambushed, Secretariat's resultant sidelong stumble ultimately forced Earl Sande to adopt a cold-blooded "kill or be killed" mentality. Already halfway out of the irons, Ron Turcotte hence had no chance when Gallant Fox was made to throw a "defensive body check".

When she saw that her rider was now lying in the middle of the strip like a piece of road-kill, a grief-stricken Penny Chenery promptly passed out. Fortunately, Lucien Laurin's left arm intervened well before Owner's Box #7's side guardrail came into play. Reacting to "Big Red's" ruin in an entirely different manner, Commander J.K.L Ross disgustedly pulled down his officer's hat and then thought, *"Serves you right you nincompoop! That's what you get for not dancing with who brought you here!"*

(Ron Turcotte would later tell the Eternity Broadcast Network's ground correspondent, "I can honestly say that the sight of Secretariat's rear end getting smaller and smaller hurt much more than my face-plant.") First waving off Jerome Park's on-call ambulatory unit, the chute's "ditched participant" next decided to release some of his pent-up frustration. Powerfully punted towards the apron, Turcotte's blue and white riding helmet ironically wound up crash landing about three feet from where one Pomeroy J. Mandalay was standing.

Aside from "Big Red's" startling disqualification, nothing thus far had come as a surprise to Eddie Arcaro. In fact, all of Frank Brunell's poker guests had clearly heard "The Master" say, "Mark my words gentlemen, Sir Barton will beat War Admiral out of the chute, not vice versa." (Of course in the here and now, Citation's prognosticating pilot only cared about sliding over so he could settle into a comfortable stalking position ahead of both Omaha and Whirlaway.)

In that he faced an extremely wide trip if nothing changed, Charlie Kurtsinger opted to prematurely activate the afterburners. Another who was also currently desperate to "save ground", Steve Cauthen thus promptly came in one lane when he realized that Jean Cruget had hastily taken off after the oval's fastest moving object. Loosening his tie as the field made their initial run past the Main Grandstand, Chic Anderson simultaneously transmitted, "War Admiral now pushes past Sir Barton two paths off the rail! One and a half lengths back to Seattle Slew! Citation strides along comfortably in fourth! Then it's three more lengths to the trio of Affirmed, Gallant Fox and Omaha! A break of four more to Assault who races in eighth position! Whirlaway is well back in ninth! Then it's Count Fleet who brings up the rear, some seventeen lengths from the front! And please be aware riders that there is a loose horse trailing the pack!"

While there was certainly no law against daydreaming, Samuel D. Riddle had never actually believed that his Champion would wind up on an uncontested lead. (Of course on the other hand, War Admiral's hard-bitten owner certainly didn't foresee this sort of scenario.) Taking his screaming jockey for a "joy ride" in the process, Sir Barton had just somehow rushed into Jerome Park's clubhouse turn a mere one-tenth of a second off of the pace!

Although it had taken him a while to make sense of things, Steve Cauthen suddenly figured out "the method to Jean Cruget's madness". Having moved in behind a speed duel that would likely butcher both parties, Seattle Slew's opportunistic jockey was therefore primed to effortlessly inherit the lead as the field turned for home. (That was of course unless someone resolved to "upset the applecart".)

Spurred by the sight of Affirmed's outstretched shadow, Seattle Slew thus snapped his head around like a Great Horned Owl who had heard a mouse run by. Extremely aggravated that his personal space had been infringed upon, Jerome Park's third place commuter consequently "got into the bit" a lot more than Jean Cruget would have liked. As a result, Charlie Kurtsinger began to "feel the squeeze" from both sides as War Admiral straightened out for his run down the backstretch.

Granted, Willie Saunders totally understood why Steve Cauthen had conducted himself the way he had. That being said, Omaha's pilot could've definitely done without the forthcoming "ripple effect". (Particularly, how the strip's "Catbird Seat" (i.e., that slot directly behind Jerome Park's four "equine-kamikazis") now belonged to none other than Citation!)

Convinced his fate was sealed if he just sat there, Saunders on that account performed a grazing "blow-past" in an effort to disrupt "Big Cy's" rhythm. (Alas, "The Master's" mount had learned exactly what not to do from a horse named Seattle Slew.) Determinedly crowding his son every step of the way, Gallant Fox's synchronized scamper compelled Chic Anderson to say, "Belair's pair now pushes forward! Citation, still unhurried, slips back to seventh!"

In that it'd been sliced clear to the bone by the back of Secretariat's right front hoof, Assault's rear left shin absolutely hurt like the dickens. Moreover, the "Club Footed Comet's" minced flesh was actively oozing pebble-sized gobs of gooey hemoglobin. (Thicker than blackstrap molasses, this red viscous runoff had now actually begun to rain down all around the dogged twosome that was tracking in ninth position.)

As he continued to endure a literal blood bath, Al Snider settled on an extremely gutsy game plan. Situated eighteen lengths back, Whirlaway no doubt had his work cut for him yet there just happened to be an unobstructed interior thoroughfare which stretched all the way to Sir Barton's chestnut derriere. Fully aware that the slightest "schematic shift" would leave him bottled up, Snider nevertheless went for broke as he made his way past the five-eighths pole.

By the time Jerome Park's far turn became relevant, some twenty-one lengths separated War Admiral and Count

Fleet. Still and all, Johnny Longden just couldn't bring himself to ask the $64,000 question. (Namely, could an accustomed frontrunner with a suspect level of fitness rally from far-far back against the Sport of Kings' best and brightest?)

Though awash with apprehension, Johnny Longden experienced a complete paradigm shift inside of that moment where Secretariat unexpectedly turned up alongside of him. See, because Jerome Park's "lone wolf" was one hundred percent recovered and had come running at full speed (seemingly in search of the lead) he was therefore the ideal entity to "slipstream" behind. *(Slipstream - Executed in all manner of racing, slipstreaming (or drafting) is when a participant purposely aligns themselves behind a competitor in order to reduce the amount of wind resistance they encounter.)* Consequently, Count Fleet was fearlessly shifted out and then vigorously roused in the wake of "Big Red's" furiously "fly by".

Right at the three-eighths marker, Charlie Kurstsinger abruptly felt War Admiral totally "bottom out". Now since he knew what his "owner's manual" said with regards to, *"If your horse completely runs out of pace...,"* Jerome Park's former top dog accordingly told himself, *"Man, stop with the whip already and just pass the torch with grace."* Obliged to convey word concerning Jerome Park's sudden "transition of power", Chic Anderson thus hotly summarized, "Sir Barton now seizes command while floating out a path! Affirmed being hard ridden ranges up into second!"

As a result of zeroing in on that thirty-six inch rift which had magically opened up along the rail, Jean Cruget's pupils grew as big as saucers. Presently sitting in third position under a tight hold, Seattle Slew simply needed a seam to jet through (yet as one might expect, Jerome Park's prime piece of real estate had suitors aplenty). Coveted also by Gallant Fox, Omaha and Whirlaway, the oval's interior artery hence became the staging area for a fierce "four-way melee".

Even though his gut prognosticated an ugly pile-up, Jean Cruget still tried to beat his three interior opponents to the punch. Swiftly and barbarously broadsided by Seattle Slew, Gallant Fox thus involuntarily bulldozed his unsuspecting offspring. Promptly pinned against the rail by all of Omaha's fifteen hundred pounds, Whirlaway subsequently decided that he would calmly "chew over the situation" with his assailant.

Once he got over the initial shock of being savagely bitten below the collar, the "Belair Bullet" began reacting to the accompanying pain. Ultimately bumped out three lanes by his son's thrashing frame, Gallant Fox in turn impeded all of Seattle Slew's forward progress. Coming away with the advantage at day's end thanks to some "dirty pool", Whirlaway thereafter blasted off towards Sir Barton with a mouth full of: flesh, blood and chestnut fur.

Seeing as how it was now "crunch time", Eddie Arcaro set out to loop the logjam which lay ahead. First making War Admiral appear as if he was standing still at a bus stop, Citation next "wiped the floor" with those who'd been compromised by "Mr. Longtail". Keeping up nicely with the ever changing complexion of Heaven's Premier Horse Race, Chic Anderson condensed a trillion thoughts and then channeled, "Sir Barton is hanging on for dear life as they hit the top of the straightaway! Affirmed to his outside is all-out in second! Whirlaway inches up on the rail in third and just like that, here comes Citation in the center of the track! He's into fourth and moving best of all!"

Because he'd cleverly ridden Secretariat's coattails, Johnny Longden was no longer able to see: Assault, War Admiral, Omaha, Gallant Fox or Seattle Slew. (Moving at the speed of sound since he didn't have to lug a 115 lb. jockey around, "Big Red" actually could have gone on to "steal the show" however the strip's solo-artist abruptly heard his conscience remind, *"Uh remember mate, no one likes a braggadocio."*) Instantly deciding that he wouldn't run down to where Secretariat had voluntary stopped, Lucien Laurin instead kept right on fanning Penny Chenery as he complimented, "Atta boy, you made your point."

Though suddenly headed in the wrong direction (because he'd "used up" too much of Affirmed on the first turn), Steve Cauthen could at least take solace in the fact that his was not the only "fruitless whip". (Specifically, since all their racers had been "roughed up" to some degree, Warren Mehrtens, Willie Saunders, Earl Sande and Jean Cruget also found themselves "lowering the boom" to no avail.) On the contrary, Whirlaway was definitely "listening" to the stick, so much so that he finally wore down Sir Barton about seventy yards past the quarter pole.

Essentially over before it began, "Mr. Longtail's" half-second reign was never even formally acknowledged. Rather, Chic Anderson appropriately announced, "Citation strikes the front with a terrific head of steam, threatening to make 2-1 look like an absolute steal!"

Despite his disappointing fall from first-place, Sir Barton kept right on swinging. Quick to realize that a certain someone was still trying to salvage a minor award, Johnny Loftus hence fully committed towards helping his old pal "hit the board". Hurriedly trading in the reins for two handfuls of slumping neck-mane, Loftus then strenuously heaved in an effort to correct his weary Champion's counterproductive running posture.

Continuing on an upswing even though he'd lost his secret weapon, Count Fleet thus soon "made casualties" out of: Affirmed, Sir Barton and Whirlaway. Now while he couldn't ever remember going this fast on horseback, Johnny Longden still knew that he had a mountain the size of Mount Everest to climb. In fact, because it measured over four lengths and there was less than an eighth of a mile to run, Citation's current advantage truly looked no less than insurmountable.

Left over from the torrential thunder shower that had rolled through at 3:30 AM, Jerome Park's last pint-sized pocket of spongy soil suddenly became relevant. Ultimately occurring fifty yards from the wire, Citation's "one-chance-in-a-million" misstep truly corresponded to a "worst case scenario" for Calumet (since it swiftly occasioned "double trouble" for one Eddie Arcaro). See, there was clearly the consequence of forfeited momentum, however then you also had everything that went along with partially tearing a right front lateral digital extensor tendon.

As he instinctively shifted his body weight over to his left leg, "The Master" commenced with nursing Citation towards the tape. Still stuck in a less than ideal situation, Johnny Longden nevertheless felt like a lotto winner the moment he recognized that Heaven's Premier Horse Race would actually come down a fifty-fifty head bob. Surprisingly presented the most even finish one could imagine, Chic Anderson therefore shook his head before he hollered, "It's too close to call!!"

241

Given that Whirlaway and Sir Barton had gone and crossed the wire four and a half lengths back of the top pair in "nose to nose" fashion, Anderson soon became guilty of sounding like a broken record. (Meaning he shouted, "...and in third it's, again folks, it's too close to call!!") Subsequently filling a good many players with fear, those five letters which spelled "PHOTO" climactically took over the tote board right as Assault brought up the rear.

In next to no time, a slow motion "stretch-replay" began looping on each of Jerome Park's elevated 60x40 meter 4k race-play video screens. (The only patron on the premises who wasn't paying attention to those images which were being shown on the infield, Adelphia Armour instead called out, "Oh waitress, please bring out a dozen magnums of your best champagne and enough glasses for this entire section!")

In spite of all the still frames and high-powered magnification lenses that they had at their disposal, it still took Leonard Jerome and August Belmont five full minutes to finalize the official running order of Heaven's Premier Horse Race. Consequent to capping a discussion about how the "Win" and "Show" photos were eerily similar, the "King of Wall Street" urged, "We should depart for the Winner's Enclosure August. On the way, I'll call these numbers in to our A/V Department."

Even though they were situated in the exact same boat, the "Managing Connections" of Citation and Count Fleet sported way different dispositions. Extraordinarily calm considering the circumstances, Warren Wright Sr. and Jimmy Jones had actually started talking with Ben Jones about Whirlaway's incredibly game performance. Conversely, Mrs. John D. Hertz and Don Cameron were trembling so bad that they could hardly breathe, never mind speak.

Like everyone else who held a "Win Ticket on #4", Pomeroy J. Mandalay had now scrutinized three slow motion replays of Citation's "star-crossed" stretch run. At day's end however, "Paradise's premier handicapper" fell into one accord with "Lady Long Shot's" latest victim. (Interrogated one replay prior by his youngest sibling, an already crestfallen Salbatore Zarcos had drunkenly stuttered, "Did he get there?! I don't know Carlos. You would have to ask either: Belmont, Jerome or Jesus.)

To no one's real surprise, a few "also-rans" totally caved into their emotions out past the wire. An outgrowth of his bitter disappointment, Charlie Kurtsinger sobbed to the extent that the racing strip could have been downgraded to sloppy! Atypically, Steve Cauthen cried like a baby too (this despite Affirmed's half-length mastery of Seattle Slew).

The fact that he bore twice the burden of anyone on horseback didn't stop one William Woodward Sr. from "lifting up" his beloved brother. Knowing from past experience that James Fitzsimmons loved to beat himself up after a loss, Belair Stud's CEO therefore consoled, "You and the boys have nothing to feel bad about Jim. Hey, we caught two terrible trips, that's horse racing."

Another owner turned comforter, Robert J. Kleberg attempted to make light of a depressing tenth place finish with some good old fashioned witticism. One who usually struck out when he wrote his own material, Assault's owner nevertheless received a teensy smile after he cracked, "C'mon Max, cheer up. Didn't you tell me in the paddock that beating Secretariat would be too wonderful for words?!"

Pretty much staying in touch during their six furlong "gallop-out", Whirlaway and Sir Barton likewise pulled up to the quarter pole within a few seconds of each other. Truly believing that he had witnessed the impossible, Al Snider for that reason complemented, "Bro let me tell you, that surpassed supernatural! I mean, no pacesetter I've rallied past has ever come back at me like that!"

While he kept one eye on the tote board, Johnny Loftus longingly sighed, "Man, when I think about all the obstacles this horse has had to overcome. Huh, believe you me Al; if he somehow lands in the money, then you will have witnessed a bona fide miracle."

After he'd thought about how Citation's rotten luck had helped him "get one over" on a certain Spaniard, Snider pointed out, "Well, yours truly received a miracle today! Who says lightning can't strike twice!?"

Instead of galloping out like he'd been told, Count Fleet had slammed on the brakes at the head of the clubhouse turn. Initially fearing the worst, Johnny Longden literally started to breathe again when he discovered that his Champion's left-front ankle was still intact. (Obviously knowing that it was a "hair either way", Mrs. John D. Hertz's racer had simply wanted to check out a high definition slow motion replay.)

Following an abbreviated quarter-mile cool down, Eddie Arcaro carefully turned his hobbled racehorse back around. Presently pessimistic about the day's pending outcome, "The Master" accordingly rejoiced when he suddenly received what looked to be a supernatural sign. Ultimately checking up right alongside Jerome Park's Winner's Enclosure, Citation almost appeared to be saying, *"Don't worry boss, we got this."*

At 6:12 PM, Jerome Park's A/V Department posted the official results of Heaven's Premier Horse Race.

$2.00 TOTE TICKETS PAY

	WIN	PLACE	SHOW
1st –	10		
2nd –	4		
3rd –	1		
4th –	2		

$2 EXACTA	–
$2 TRIFECTA	–
$2 SUPERFECTA	–
$.10 SUPERFECTA	–

In back of descending from "Cloud 9", Johnny Longden ecstatically wrapped his arms around Count Fleet's lathered neck. Weeping for joy as he showered the "last horse standing" with loads of loving kisses, Jerome Park's prevailing jockey only stopped in order to scream, "Who's the best?! That's right boy! You are!"

Upon learning his fate, Eddie Arcaro dejectedly dismounted from the day's runner-up. Quick to offer an apology, "The Master" continued to stroke Citation's snout as he spilled, "My fault pal. I slept in when I should have been out walking the strip."

With zero hesitation, Warren Wright Sr., Jimmy Jones and Ben Jones rushed in to sincerely congratulate Count Fleet's rhapsodic Connections. In the same way, adulation sprung forth from every corner of Section 2A right up until that time when a squadron of policemen made the scene. Eventually wreathed by their formal escort, Mr. and Mrs. John D. Hertz, Don Cameron, Stan Martin and Mr. Sam were then pointed in the direction of Jerome Park's prepped Winner's Enclosure.

In celebration of Sir Barton "winning the bronze", Johnny Loftus jubilantly fired three punches into the air. Compelled to vigorously applaud, Al Snider simultaneously complemented, "I take my hat off to you guys Johnny. You both ran a marvelous race."

For obvious reasons, Pomeroy J. Mandalay wanted to "get out of Dodge" before the Winner's Enclosure's forthcoming ceremony got underway. Now since he felt like he'd been socked in the gut with a sledgehammer, Jerome Park's second evacuee indeed welcomed the comic relief that soon came via another ruined risk taker. Climbing into a cab on the other side of the turnstiles, Commander J.K.L. Ross cordially waved and then yelled, "Hey Pomeroy, care to split a fare?! Goodness knows we could both use the five bucks!"

Although the sight of Section 1C's "champagne party" truly made him sick, Salbatore Zarcos was actually way more upset about losing his secondary bet. Why you ask? Well, unlike Paradise's preeminent proposition wager, the purchase of pari-mutual ticket "#777564128" had not been a calculated risk. Rather, it was the reckless offshoot of drinking way too much red "extra fruity" sangria.

As the vanquished were led back through the gap courtesy of their respective grooms, Johnny Longden embarked on a "victory cantor" past the Main Grandstand. Promptly electing to add some "bells and whistles" to this proceeding, Jesus Christ thus spoke to that patch of sky which crowned Jerome Park's straightaway. Rearing up first to show his love for the *One* who had created him, Count Fleet then completed his "curtain call" beneath a down pouring of red roses, Black-Eyed Susans and white carnations.

In that the day had produced a most improbable result, winning pari-mutual tickets were "rarer then hen's teeth". Nevertheless, not a single one of Leonard Jerome's foiled guests mistook the ground for a waste receptacle. (There was a widening epidemic of envy however thanks to a certain composition of pari-mutual prices which had appeared.)

			WIN	PLACE	SHOW
1st	–	10	$65.20	$31.40	$17.60
2nd	–	4		$7.00	$5.20
3rd	–	1			$15.80
4th	–	2			

$2 EXACTA	–	$394.60
$2 TRIFECTA	–	$17,939.40
$2 SUPERFECTA	–	$125,017.20
$.10 SUPERFECTA	–	$12,501.72

The first to welcome Jerome Park's conquering heroes into the Winner's Enclosure, August Belmont thereupon draped Count Fleet with the Tri-Floral Winner's Garland. Similarly, Lady Randolph Churchill immediately started distributing robust bouquets of red roses, Black-Eyed Susans and white carnations to: Johnny Longden, Mr. & Mrs. John D. Hertz, Don Cameron, Stan Martin and Mr. Sam. Charged with bestowing the Rex Equos, Leonard Jerome next proceeded with Count Fleet's coronation while he cried, "Hear ye hear ye, all hail the king of horses!"

Since Mrs. John D. Hertz was adamant about including the "King of Wall Street" and August Belmont in the official winner's snapshot, Jerome Park's sanctioned photographer was forced to "hold the phone" for a few minutes. Finally getting her wish after quite the struggle, Count Fleet's triumphant owner then chuckled, "Gosh, I think this is the least I can do considering the dinner y'all fed me last night!"

In the wake of his "flying dismount", Johnny Longden ran over and affectionately "bear-hugged" Don Cameron. Once this highly emotional scene had played out, the Eternity Broadcast Network's ground correspondent got the ball rolling with, "Uh please, Mr. Jerome, now before we hear from the winning Connections, what are your thoughts on today's record breaking turnout?"

As he continued to choke back his tears, the principal host of Heaven's Premier Horse Race elegantly articulated, "What can I say except; thank you Horse Racing

Nation, for making every dream I've ever had come true a thousand times over!"

Following a full two minute ovation, the Winner's Enclosure's emcee turned his attention towards the "woman of the hour". Promptly asked the exact question she had prepared for, Mrs. John D. Hertz hence recited, "Did we get a little lucky? Sure we did. At the same time, let's credit Count Fleet for putting himself in a position where he could actually get lucky."

Subconsciously putting an arm around both Stan Martin and Mr. Sam as he was singled out, Jerome Park's winning jockey soon hearkened unto, "Tell me Mr. Longden, since you were ultimately able to slipstream behind Secretariat, was your mount's tardy beginning a blessing in disguise?"

Without thinking twice, the Eternity Broadcast Network's current interviewee answered, "It was definitely a blessing for the reason you mentioned, but more so because I truly believe that a spirited start would have caused us to reach the strip's spongy spot ahead of Citation."

Whereas the media had called his unorthodox training methodology into question on more than one occasion, it was assumed that Don Cameron would now "have a word" for his critics. Yet, when the "mic" finally came his way, the Winner's Enclosure's reining conditioner had nothing to say except, "For weeks to come I'll likely hear and read about what a great horseman I am. However like I've always said, 'A great horseman is simply the byproduct of a great racehorse.'"

www.ingramcontent.com/pod-product-compliance
Lightning Source LLC
Chambersburg PA
CBHW070859250626
47159CB00003B/1118